Fat, Ugly, Stupid

Chapter 1 – Fifteen 1976

"Fat, ugly, stupid!" the boy, Steve, said scornfully as the noise of the school corridor instantly quietened and the words rang out like church bells. He was lounging nonchalantly with his back to the window on the landing by the sixth-form common room. The small hairs forming the outer edge of his mid-length blonde, wavy hair glowed in a shaft of sunlight, creating a halo effect around his head. In contrast his blue eyes were cold as he met Laura's gaze and brutally summarised his feelings towards her as she reached the top of the stairs, blithely unaware that she was walking towards a new part of her life. The part where her insouciant teenage self-worth heard the death knell and fears and anxieties took over her life. His glamorous friends, a mix of girls and boys, laughed unkindly then ran off down the corridor towards the library, shoes slapping noisily on the tiles, their voices echoing as they shouted joyously at each other. Not one of them gave a second thought to the person who had been the butt of the cruelty and most of them never thought of that moment again. The whole episode lasted no more than a few seconds but to Laura time ground to a halt as she stood in front of the juvenile judge and his sycophantic jury whilst he summed her whole being up in those three small words. She understood what it meant to want the earth to open up and swallow her whole but, unobligingly, it didn't and she had to suffer the humiliation like a nasty dose of medicine. Never before had she thought of herself as fat, ugly or stupid but she did then. The words so shocked her that they carved themselves into her brain. She felt betrayed and utterly bereft, her previously innocent and carefree life instantly meaningless and empty. She was only 15 but she knew, with utmost certainty that the moment would define the rest of her life.

Chapter 2 – Fifteen

Three months beforehand, Laura had been sat behind Steve for Maths, a subject that she had little interest in thanks to a teacher with the charisma of a conker. Outside the sky was deep blue and the leaves on the tree tops waved gracefully in appreciation of the warm sunny day. Some 5th year boys were playing cricket on the playing field. They were dressed in an assortment of white and off-white T-shirts and shorts with the odd black pair thrown in. Periodically a thwack could be heard as one of the batsmen finally connected with the hard red ball and a faint shout with an instruction to run or stay put could be heard on the breeze.

Sometimes the play stopped and the teacher intervened to explain a point or rule that had just arisen out of a piece of play. Further around the field the 5th year girls were playing rounders, their pony-tailed hair shining in the sun. She wished she was out there bowling a quick ball or athletically jumping high in the air like the bionic woman to make a catch, the whole team clapping her on the back as she won the game for her team. A plane droned overhead. The teacher's voice droned in the class room.

"So, what is the answer, Laura?" said Mr Lewis, the ancient, 37-year-old, maths teacher in a sarcastic tone "Is it lbw or a no ball?"

Laura was startled out of her reverie. She sat up and looked at the blackboard covered with white chalk marks of x's and y's and equals signs and wracked her brains for a witty answer.

"Actually, I was watching the rounders and the answer is X squared minus 2Y, Sir"

or

"Not sure about the lbw, could have been edged, Sir, 2x-y is the answer" cue admiring glances from the rest of the class.

None of that happened.

"Uh, ummmm" She dithered and felt her face flush as blood rushed to the surface of her skin. She stared at her blank exercise book with its neat grid lines.

"I'm waiting" said Mr Lewis impatiently in a threatening voice. He was a small scruffy man with a comb-over and a thin menacing moustache, who made up for his lack of height with a sharp tongue and a reputation for bullying.

The boy in front dropped his pencil and bent down to pick it up, as he did so he whispered,

"X squared divided by 2". He didn't look at her and she didn't betray that she had heard anything although it didn't fool Mr, bat-ears, Lewis.

"X squared divided by 2" Laura replied trying to look as if she had given it some thought.

"That is correct, Laura" said the bat-eared one with exaggerated patience "but you are not always going to be fortunate enough to have somebody sitting in front of you to help every time you come up against a problem. Paying attention would be much more beneficial." Smug attitude intact he turned back to the board and began writing. Laura wished she could come up with a witty repost.

Twenty minutes later the bell rang and the torturous lesson was over. Laura stood up, pushed her chair back with her legs and started to pack her bag as did the boy in front. She knew his name and that he was in another of the top stream forms. All the forms amalgamated for lessons and were put into sets according to their ability. She had no idea why she had been put in the top set for maths as it interested her about as much as watching the playing field grass grow. If she shone at all it was more in English where she could write a lot of waffle and refer to a couple of Shakespearian quotes to earn a C. She spoke "Thanks for that, I had no idea what the answer was".

"That was obvious" Steve said with a grin "No problem. You want to be careful though, that little sadist will have it in for you from now on". He shouted at a tall dark-haired boy who was heading to the door "Al, oy, Al. Wait for me" threw his satchel over his shoulder and with his shirt tails hanging out of his trousers, was gone.

Chapter 3 – Fifteen

The next week the little sadist wasn't waiting to start the lesson and as the minutes dragged on the noise level in the classroom got louder. Steve swung around in his chair and sat sideways on to his desk idly dapping a tennis ball on the floor. "Do you like cricket?" He asked looking around at Laura.

Laura was surprised to be asked but didn't let it show. Steve had sat in front of her for a few months now but had only recently started making the odd comment to her. Their social spheres were worlds apart and she hadn't been prepared for a full-blown conversation.

"Dad watches it and he's tried to teach me the rules but it is a bit slow and boring – nothing happens for ages then when something does, they all shout 'Jolly good shot' and 'bravo' like a bunch of braying donkeys. It's just that what's going on out there is more interesting than what is going on in here".

Steve laughed.

"Well, Maths is one of my favourite subjects, but I know what you mean. You ought to pay attention, though, you might need it one day."

Laura wrinkled her nose in horror. "I doubt it. I hate being inside on a nice day especially when we've got that creep". She gestured towards the blackboard where Mr Lewis should be standing. "Wouldn't you rather be out there?"

"Yes, but when we've got English Lit. It's so boring, all that Shakespeare 'Though art, aren't though' crap. What the hell is a Midsummer Night's Dream about, anyway? Can you see the back of my blazer?" Steve pointed at his jacket hung on the back of the chair. "that's where Miss Sandall threw the board rubber at me last week – it takes ages for the chalk to come out. Mum nearly killed me when she saw it".

They laughed companionably. He chatted on about the subjects that he liked. Biology and Physics, typical boy's stuff, nothing she was remotely interested in or good at but she liked the sound of his voice and the feeling of inclusion. He had blonde wavy hair and blue eyes with the lithe body that comes with youth and was built for playing sport. When Mr Lewis finally entered the room and started the lesson, Steve turned around to face forward and she noticed his slim back and the way his hair curled just over the collar of his white school shirt.

Maths became a less dreaded lesson – she couldn't get excited about the subject but if she got picked upon again Steve found a way of helping her by writing the answer at the bottom of his page and easing it over to the side of the desk so that she could see it. They had one other lesson together and that was chemistry but she sat at one end of the lab and he, the other, although through the sea of pupils she could see his face and sometimes catch his eye, he rarely looked in her direction and did not acknowledge her if he did. She wasn't bothered. She had Maths.

One Thursday afternoon the top three forms of the 4th year girls were queuing up on one side of a corridor outside the changing rooms waiting to go out to play rounders. They lounged against the scuffed and dirty brown-painted wall talking about television and the pop charts when the boys ran past laughing and shouting in high spirits on their way to play football. Their studs clattered noisily on the stone floor competing with their exaggerated bantering and cheeky comments aimed at their female audience. The smell of testosterone and Brut aftershave filled the air. As he ran past Steve winked in her direction and Laura blushed.

In the sunshine at lunchtime Laura sat with her friends, Jane and Sally, in a corner of the playing field chatting and sunbathing. She had been to the shop outside of the school gates and spent her dinner money on a packet of crisps and a mars bar, as usual, and was happy. Her mother would not have been had she known.

"Have you heard who Sharon is going out with?" asked Jane shading her eyes from the sun "Mark – Mark Singleton" She continued before anybody had had a chance to answer.

"No!" exclaimed Sally who was sat cross-legged on the grass. "I can't believe that. I thought he was mad on Sandra – the one from 4B not 4M".

"He was but she fancies Steve Miles so wouldn't give him the time of day" replied Jane enjoying the gossip.

Steve Miles! Laura had been lying with her eyes closed, hands folded across her chest, absorbing all the rays that she could. Her ears pricked up and she hoisted herself onto one elbow, squinting in the sunshine and asked as casually as she could "Does he fancy her?".

"I don't think so" carried on Jane who seemed to be in the know about everybody's love lives. "Rumour has it he fancies somebody else but nobody can get him to admit who". Laura settled back on the grass, closed her eyes and, at peace with the world, was content to listen to her friends gossip on.

When she got off the bus after school and walked down the road and into her driveway her mother was sat in the garden, wearing a big straw hat and a yellow sun dress. She had been reading but looked up and greeted her daughter with a wave and a smile. She seemed happy so Laura went over and sat beside her on a tartan travel rug that was laid out on the grass. She guessed her father was coming home that night and their latest fight had been resolved. This was good news; the house would be a home again for a few days.

"How was school?" her mother asked.

"Not bad – normal. You know." Laura laid back on the blanket with her knees bent up towards the sun and shielded her eyes with her arm.

"Do you have any homework?" her mother grilled.

"Yes, maths and history. I don't have a clue about the maths. Do you think you could take a look?"

Her mother laughed. Laura laughed, too. They both knew her mother's lightning speed at calculating a discount on a dress but complete lack of awareness when it came to balancing the household books. Or at least that was what she led people to believe. She elegantly side-stepped the question.

"It's years since I did any maths and it's all changed since my day. That's your father's thing. Don't you have any friends that can help you?"

Laura shrugged, sighed and got up to go into the house. She didn't want to ask if her father was definitely going to be there that night because it affected her mother's mood and she didn't want to change that whilst she seemed to be in a good one.

"I've made your favourite cake. If you want a slice, it's in the tin" her mother called as she picked up her sunglasses and went back to her book "Oh, and change out of your uniform, I'm not putting the washing machine on until the weekend."

The kitchen smelt of casserole and there was a vanilla cheesecake from a packet in the fridge. Laura concluded that her father would be there for dinner, helped herself to the cake and went up to her room. She wasn't going to ask him about the maths homework and she wasn't going to do it.

Chapter 4 – Fifteen

It was coming up to exam time so in preparation there were tests in every subject. Day after day of tests. Laura thought they would never end. Biology 4/10, Physics 3/10, English Literature 9/10, History 7/10 and then there was Maths.

The classroom was hot and stuffy with only two small windows letting in a slight warm breeze when the outside air stirred. Laura had no idea how Mr Lewis managed to make his voice so monotone. Did he practice? She could imagine him boring his obviously saint-like little wife into a coma. "Enid" he would say "is this dull enough?" and she would reply "Not quite, love, slow it down a tad. Yes, that's it you've got it zzzzz".

"Question no 4 – look at the equation on the board and work out what x should be – you have 5 minutes." If she had had 5 hours it wouldn't have made any difference, Laura thought. She guessed a number and waited for the others to finish. At the desk in front of her Steve was writing assiduously, clearly understanding what needed to be done and doing it. She looked at the curls on his collar and wondered what it would be like to run her fingers through them.

"Question no 5," said Mr Lewis.

Laura knew the answer to that question. There were some parts of maths that she did understand, not much, just a little, the bits that she thought might be useful. Her mind began to wander again and she gazed at the white-shirted back in front of her willing him to turn around and smile at her. She could smell his body in the heat, sweat, soap and sunshine. It filled her nostrils and coursed through her body to every nerve ending it could find. She began to daydream of she and Steve together, somewhere, anywhere. He was gazing into her eyes, desire radiating from them. He bent over to kiss her on the lips and the jolt of raw sexual hunger this provoked brought Laura out of her reverie and into the present. This boy, man, boy sat in front of her was THE one. The one she would yield everything to, the one she craved, the one she wanted. Suddenly she felt grown up, an adult. An adult that wanted to lie naked next to another person. The sudden onset of unadulterated desire took her by surprise. She had had phases of loving rabbits, then ponies then Les McKeown from the Bay City Rollers but until then boys had never interested her. But, this one did. She knew with certainty that this was no passing fancy, no five-minute wonder, this was a love that would last.

Inwardly delirious with her new found happiness she started to doodle at the bottom of her page LC 4 SM with a heart around it. Then she added the word 'ever' under the 4 with an arty swirl.

"Question no 6," said Mr Lewis.

An interminable twenty minutes later Laura had actually managed to answer 5 out of the 15 questions and had guessed the rest. She couldn't see the point of doing the subject as she didn't envisage a career when she would ever need it. Not that she really knew what she was going to do. She supposed it would be something to do with writing, or reading books. She wasn't really sure what but numbers did not figure in her occasional vague ponderings on her future or when her father brought the subject up at the dinner table on the days he ate at home.

"So, Laura, have you given any thought to your future?" He had asked the last time picking up pieces of meat and cabbage with his fork and placing them carefully in his mouth. He asked this question at least once a month and Laura got extremely bored of answering it. She wasn't sure how many more ways there were to say no, she had no idea what she was going to do.

"Not really, Dad" She also forked food into her mouth to prevent her having to say much more "I'm just focusing on the exams at the moment. The teachers are working us pretty hard. Tests nearly every lesson – you know."

"You should join me - become an accountant. It's a good career and well paid. Your mother doesn't have to work".

In a good mood with her husband her mother nodded in acquiescence forgetting how bored she was half the time and how much she wished that she did have to work in order to fill her day.

Laura had no intention of becoming an accountant. She knew one thing about accounts, it meant numbers and numbers meant maths –

something which she could not get her head around. To pacify her father, she made up some lies about looking into becoming a journalist and he changed the subject to the new prime minister, James Callaghan's politics and she was off the hook.

Back in the classroom she heard a voice.

"Have you all finished?" asked the hirsute sadistic bat-eared one "Well, swap your paper with the person in front and you can mark each other's work – it will save me a job" Mr Lewis laughed mirthlessly but nobody else joined in. Out of the corner of her eye Laura saw a piece of paper balanced on her shoulder from the boy behind and as she moved her hand to retrieve it, Steve swung around and grabbed her test before she gave it a thought.

Chapter 5 – Fifteen

Laura could hear a girl screaming and she wasn't sure if it was on the bus radio or in her head. It was supposed to be a pop song but it was just one endless scream! There was more screaming, though, and that was definitely in her head.

What was the point of demoting her to the lower set in Maths with three weeks to go before the exam? Her father would not be happy. For a change she hoped that he wasn't going to be around for a while. She would tolerate her mother's bad mood; anything was better than the lecture she would inevitably get from him. That was not really what her head noise was about, though, it was the way Steve had slammed her test paper back onto her desk, thrown his books into his satchel and stalked off without a backward glance. She looked at the paper – he had written one letter on it, right at the bottom. Right where she had doodled something that she really wished she hadn't. It was an N.

She had been mortified when she realised that he would see what she had drawn. At no point had Mr Lewis said that they would mark each other's papers she was sure of that. If she had known then she would never have written on the bottom. As the marking started and Steve hadn't moved or made any comment, she harboured a tiny hope that he wouldn't mind, that it was the little hint that he needed to make a throwaway remark to her about walking her to the bus or meeting up at the weekend to go to the cinema. She watched his subsequent actions as if it was an out of body experience, her mortification hundred times worse than it had been in the minutes before. Like a zombie she collected her pens from the desk and put them in the pocket of her satchel, gradually becoming aware of a voice calling her. Bewildered, she walked towards the front of the classroom and stood in front of Mr Lewis's desk. She heard the words, 'demoted', 'Class 2' and 'for the best' then zombie-like she walked out of the school to the bus queues. As she dropped into the seat on the coach the events of the last few minutes caught up with Laura as her head started to throb and a searing pain formed in her throat as she fought hard to not to cry.

Laura stepped off the bus when it stopped and walked down the road. She could see that her mother's bedroom curtains were drawn which meant she had a migraine and wouldn't want to be disturbed. She was glad, she knew her mother would have to know about the class demotion but she was just not in the mood to tell her. In the kitchen she put a piece of cake and an apple on a plate, filled a glass with squash and went to her room. On the way she gently knocked on her mother's door to let her know she was home. Things had to stay as normal. She needed time to think and did not want to alert her mother to anything being wrong. The last thing she needed right then was the third degree about her future.

Shafts of sunlight filtered in across the yellow candlewick bedspread as she threw herself down on the bed giving vent to the emotions that had been building up in her for the last never-ending hour. She stifled her sobs in the pillow, her body wracking with the silent crying until it hurt. She felt a fool and the more she went over the classroom scenario in her head the more her face burned and the stupider she felt. She didn't understand Steve's reaction. They got along, didn't they? He was the one that had instigated the initial conversation. He had seemed interested in her. Why was declaring her interest back such a bad thing? Jane and Sally had said he fancied a secret somebody. Couldn't it have been her?

An interminable weekend went by. Laura lurched between hope and despair, replaying the events of Friday afternoon over and over in her head. She'd misunderstood, hadn't she? He had been in a hurry and hadn't wanted to speak. There was one thing that she could not wipe out of her memory and that was the letter that he had added to her paper. There was no misconstruing that.

On Monday morning at school Laura watched Steve from a distance whilst she stood with her friends in the playground waiting for the bell to go. Jane and Sally chatted about their weekend oblivious to her mood. He seemed fine, surrounded by a group of boys in various stages of dishevelment despite the time of day. They laughed and joked and kicked a tennis ball around the floor between them pushing each other off balance in order to be the one to get to it. Laura couldn't help observing how little it took to keep them amused.

Periods 3 and 4 meant chemistry and now that they no longer had maths together this was her only chance of redeeming things. She had a plan; she would casually glance in his direction and smile. A friendly smile, open, happy. A smile that said she wasn't bothered by what had happened on Friday. That she was a cool person and she would be a good choice of girlfriend. She would forgive his reaction – it was to be expected. He was a little shocked but had now had time to get used to the suggestion and it wasn't such a bad one. They could go back to their jokey companionability. It would work out, she was sure.

The class filed in to the lab and took up their usual seats on the high wooden stools. Mr Macmillan wrote a couple of acronyms from the periodic table and asked if anyone knew what they were. Already Laura had switched off and instead of focusing on the class, casually lifted her head and looked in Steve's direction, her face deliberately impassive as if she had forgotten he took this class with her but ready to smile warmly when he caught her eye. He had beaten her to it. He was already looking at her but it wasn't a conspiratorial look of fond resignation, it was a stare – a long cold baleful stare. It held such venom that Laura began to feel uncomfortable. He didn't blink or move his head and eventually she had to look away her face growing puce with embarrassment. She was left in no doubt that they were no longer friends. More than that he hated her and she felt as if the punishment did not fit the crime. Was liking somebody so bad? Was this what happened if you got it wrong? She learnt nothing of the elements in the classroom that day but everything about how painful unrequited love could be.

On the bus that morning she had been thinking about a book she was reading. It was a romance. Boy meets girl, boy does something stupid and loses girl, girl realises that she loves boy anyway. Happy ever after. She was hoping that could happen in real life, too. She now knew it would never happen to her. She was not that type of girl.

As Laura reached the top of the stairs, after lunch, she recognised a couple of Steve's friends standing by the window at the end of the upstairs corridor. It had been too late to avoid them so she had stared at the floor and tried to become invisible, attempting to slide by without being noticed. The boys were hanging out with some of the cool girls that weren't friends of Laura. They were laughing, engrossed in their own world with the assured confidence that attractive teenagers emit. She envied their poise, slim, willowy bodies and long glossy hair. Their school uniforms adapted to look fashionable enhanced the glamorous look. They had an ability to make every situation belong to them. To not know what it was like to struggle for friendship, intelligence even love. Lost in her own thoughts it didn't occur to Laura until she analysed the whole scenario over and over in her head afterwards that they were giggling and talking about her and that the words she was hearing were meant for her. Laura's stomach had clenched as the teenagers all turned to look in her direction making her the centre of attention that she had desperately tried to avoid. There, stood in the middle of the group had been Steve, staring directly at her, and from his sneering mouth came the words that had stuck like a record in her head. One second of humiliation, a life sentence of self-loathing and the glossy girls had laughed.

Chapter 6 – Fifteen

Nothing about Steve's looks had ever concerned him one way or another. He could not identify good looks in a man so did not know whether he was pleasing to the female eye or not. He was really not all that bothered because he was popular. He was outgoing and friendly and had a little circle of male friends who lived in the local streets where they played football in the evenings. He didn't pay a lot of attention to girls, if they were around and he knew them he would speak but if not, he just got on with his day. Later in life somebody had told him that he was self-involved but he didn't care what other people thought!

Steve's upbringing had been loving but uneventful. His father worked as a manager in the local meat factory and his mother as a dinner lady at the primary school he had attended. It was the ideal job as she could be at home with the children in the holidays. Money had never been plentiful but he and his younger brother had not lacked for anything. His parents being the type to put their offspring's needs above their own. They went on holiday to the seaside once a year and otherwise led a routine life. As he hit the tricky teenage years, Steve, became arrogant and unruly. His parents were not well equipped to discipline a fast-growing, fast-thinking teenager and gave in to a lot of his demands in the hope of an easy life. They naively concluded that if he had what he wanted it would bring the best out of him but it didn't quite work like that. Instead, Steve became shallow and uncaring, lacking in empathy and emotion. He lost respect for his parents and treated them with ill-disguised contempt. They never admitted this to anybody not even each other and away from the house Steve learnt to use charm to get what he wanted out of life.

One summer evening Lorraine, a pretty girl with long blonde hair sat herself down on a low wall near where he and his friends were playing football and thumbed through a fashion magazine. She paid no attention to Steve or anybody else but he took an interest. After 15 minutes of sly sideways glances without a flicker in return, he pretended to miss a kick so the ball would roll past him towards the wall and he would have to retrieve it. He put a hand up as an apology to the lads and ran languidly to get the football.

"Sorry, didn't mean to disturb you" he said as a means of opening a conversation. She looked up, the mascara and eye liner she was wearing made her eyes sparkle.

"You're not" she said coolly.

"What are you reading?" he asked not wanting to walk away now he had her attention. "Company – I'm not really reading it – just looking at the fashion pages". She showed him an upside-down page full of brightly coloured dresses.

He couldn't think of anything more boring but wasn't going to give up an opportunity to spend some time with her. His friends were getting impatient, yelling at him to bring the ball back.

"Give me ten more minutes and I'll join you" he said with a grin and kicked the football back up the street.

It had become a regular thing. Once or twice a week Lorraine would perch on the low wall, wearing a different selection of the most up-to-the minute fashion items and a variety of coloured eye-shadows, while Steve played football and did his best to show off. Afterwards, they would chat and he would walk her back to her house. Sometimes, if it was chilly, he would offer her his denim jacket to wrap around her shoulders. It was slightly too big and smelt of Denim aftershave and deodorant. He didn't touch her or kiss her or even hold her hand but bided his time knowing that treating a girl with respect yielded results.

One night, as they sat on the wall, she said "So, you've got an admirer, then?"

"I have?" he was surprised "who?"

"Come on" Lorraine said flirtatiously confident in the knowledge that she was the only one he was interested in "don't tell me you don't know?"

Steve thought for a minute. He couldn't think of anybody so shook his head. "No, I've got no idea".

Lorraine looked sideways at him and realised that he genuinely didn't have a clue.

"Laura Coombs" she waited for a reaction.

Again, he looked puzzled. "Laura Coombs?"

"Oh, come on, Steve. Don't be so dumb. I thought you sat by her for maths"

A light pinged on in Steve's head "The thick one that sits behind me? Her?"

Lorraine was bored with the game now and scuffed the toe of her shoe on the grass "Yes, Steve – her. I thought you might be amused".

"Amused? Why would I want to go out with somebody like her?"

The implication being that he had Lorraine and wanted no-one else. This was exactly what she had wanted to hear so having the little boost to her ego that she needed said mischievously.

"Then, maybe you should make that clear".

The ridiculous doodle on the test sheet a few days later convinced him that she was right. He would be very clear.

Chapter 7 – Twenty-five 1986

Laura moved the umbrella around a little to block out the sun from her eyes and picked up the magazine again. She didn't read a lot of magazines preferring a decent thriller or literature such as Jane Austen. She found it a good antidote to staring at figures all day. The only reason she had bought it was because of the headline screaming at her from the news-stand, '6 easy ways to a flat stomach'. She couldn't resist finding out all she could. There was nothing new in the article – she didn't expect there to be but she just had to be sure. She already did 400 sit-ups a day and avoided nuts and chips and chocolate like the plague. The rest of the issue was filled with cake recipes, fashion, knitting patterns and a highly entertaining problems page. Did men really keep women's clothing in the potting shed to dress up in or women yearn to be ravished by the vicar? She dropped the magazine onto the sand and laid back with her eyes closed. A transistor radio played Chain Reaction by Diana Ross further down the beach, the waves gently washed onto the shore with a shushing noise and the gulls called plaintively to each other as they wheeled overhead looking for discarded sandwiches on the beach. Laura felt languorous and relaxed as she closed her eyes for a nap. Steven would be back from his walk to the bar soon so she took the opportunity while she could.

She didn't nap though. Once her eyes were closed and she started to drift off, like a vivid technicolour film inside her head the scene from the morning on the school landing played itself out again. As real in her head as it had been 10 years beforehand. In truth she didn't think of it a lot, it was a painful memory like getting stung by a wasp or cut with a knife. She shut it into a cupboard in her head, locked the door and metaphorically hid the key. Her life was busy and full so the key only got used when she was feeling low (or on a happy holiday it seemed!) but when it did there were no fuzzy edges. Time had not dimmed the excruciating humiliation that had washed over her on that day. Humiliation, it turned out, took a long time to recover from even if it spurred you on to become a better version of yourself. With the benefit of hindsight, she realised that in one split second her life had both ended and started again.

At the time she had been temporarily rooted to the spot her face burning with embarrassment as the group ran away. Utterly bewildered and looking like a rabbit in headlights she had pushed through the group of bystanders as they gawped silently at her.

She recalled little about the rest of the day but she did remember the feeling of complete emptiness that had descended over her. The initial feelings of hurt and betrayal gave way to despair. Nothing mattered any more. She had been 15 years old and nothing had mattered that day, the next day or at the weekend. She had tried to think of the future but it had felt like a big black gaping chasm rolling out in front of her with nothing in it. Would she still feel this way when she was 30 or 40? Would she feel this empty and foolish for the rest of her life. She didn't know. She had had 15 years of relative happiness to go on. Nothing had prepared her for another person treating her as if she was a discarded cigarette butt. Something that could be tossed down and ground into the floor without a second thought.

At home, after dinner, Laura had escaped to her bedroom away from her mother's well-meant attentions. She had recovered enough from her migraine to cook a light tea and to work out that something was wrong. Laura barely ate; she still had a sick feeling in the pit of her stomach and tried hard to convince her mother that it was just the pressure of school work. She wasn't fooled but got the message that Laura needed to be left alone.

    Finally getting some privacy Laura had faced the full-length mirror and taken off all of her clothes. She had stared at herself in a way she never had before. Was she fat? Was she ugly? Nobody had ever said anything so mortifying to her before. She was shocked. She scrutinised herself. Her arms and her legs had tan lines from wearing short sleeved shirts and shorts in the sunshine but they were slim with the muscularity of youth. Her shoulders were square and didn't slope, her breasts were small mounds and her stomach was rounded and stuck out as if she was newly pregnant. She turned around and looked over her shoulder to examine her bottom. It was flabby with no definition between it and her thighs and there were a few dimples on the cheeks. She didn't know what to make of her pubic area (was that what people referred to their own genitalia as?) – she had nothing to compare it with. A few hairs grew at the top of her sturdy thighs and made her feel untidy and scruffy-looking.

She had examined her head. Long straight hair that descended down her back in a mousy brown colour framed a square face with heavy eyebrows and bright blue eyes. She felt her nose was a bit too big for her face and there were a few hairs growing in the moustache area. When had all of that happened? She hadn't noticed. Laura opened her mouth and found that her teeth were white and even. She forced herself to smile and even though she was doing it for no reason her face transformed and lit up. Laura saw it differently; she saw a horse; an unattractive equine staring back at her. In horror she had realised that Steve was right, she was ugly. She turned away from the mirror with tears in her eyes.

She didn't have to examine inside her head – she was clearly stupid! And she was fat and she was ugly. As her mood darkened, she thought bitterly that at least the opposite sex would never be a problem and she could do whatever she wanted with her life! But she hadn't known what that was and it hadn't made her feel better. She had wanted to fit in, be popular, have boys fancy her. She had wanted to get married, maybe have children, be a 'glossy' girl. But now she knew she was kidding herself; she was always going to be a freak. A girl that would forever be looking in from the outside with her nose pressed against the window. She just wished somebody had warned her. That night she had silently sobbed herself to sleep for the first time of many.

Her mother had not been impressed with the way Laura had started to push her food around the plate. She had tried to think of the starving children as had been suggested but, honestly, they could have her food. The tiny bits she did eat got stuck on the large lump in her throat. Laura couldn't tell her what had happened. Well, she could have done and her mother would have sympathised and told her to ignore bullies and that life went on, that she would be fine, blah, blah! Mums seemed to have a dictionary of platitudes to roll out for every occasion.

She didn't want to hear any of them. She would not have understood that Laura had found the one person, the only person, she would ever want for the whole of her life and that he hated her. Then her mother would have said not to talk nonsense, that she was only young and that she couldn't possibly know her own mind at the age of 15. So, Laura hadn't said anything – there had been no point.

Her small group of friends had struggled with her, too. It had got around the whole school that popular Steve Miles had embarrassed poor little Laura Coombs in front of everybody. They had rallied around and tried to reassure her that what he said wasn't true, that he was a bully and that insults were just words and couldn't hurt. That had been easy to say – it hadn't been aimed at them and they were wrong the words had hurt like hell.

She felt something cold against her leg which jolted her back to the present and Steven's voice said "I brought you a sparkling water – thought you might be hot".

She thanked him and agreed that, yes, she was hot. After all, she thought cynically, heat normally comes with sun! But she didn't say it out loud. She had decided that this could be the one; as close to her type as she was going to get. She didn't want to ruin anything. This was their first holiday together and they were giving it a trial to see how being in each other's company solidly 24/7 for a week worked out.

Steven laid out on the sun bed beside her and closed his eyes. She took this as a signal that he was happy to just do nothing in her company for a while so she shut hers, again, too.

In 1976 the summer holidays had finally come along and she had been glad to be out of the goldfish bowl of school where she felt people were whispering about her when she walked past and talking about her behind her back. Jane and Sally had been the most supportive, trying to shield her from the worst of the gossip and on one occasion that Laura wasn't supposed to know about physically intimidating a girl they had found scrawling something unspeakable about her on the toilet wall. She had felt like a freak. She had been labelled the worst of the worst on every level and it made her feel worthless. What was the point of going to school or learning anything if a few small words could take away all your self-esteem in a fraction of a second, rendering your life a joke? The months of July and August had stretched out ahead of her like a big buffer distancing her from the gossip and the sniggering. She hoped that she would be old news by the time school resumed in September. The last year she would have to attend and she was determined to make it the last year that she would attend.

Two weeks into the holidays and bored with her mother's company and the endless round of chores Laura was expected to do she listlessly picked up a magazine from the glass-topped coffee table in the living room. She took it out into the garden and laid out on the travel rug spread on the lawn. The day was hot with a cloudless blue sky and the sun beat down. Flipping through the articles Laura was surprised to find no fashion pages or recipes and double took the cover. The picture was of a young woman wearing a fitted cream shirt and a mid-length brown skirt. She was gazing defiantly down the lens of the camera with her arms folded. The headline screamed 'Material gains' and the story was of the young lady's success at turning around an out-of-favour fashion house into a profitable business once more. Laura realised that instead of reading one of her mother's publications it was one that belonged to her father. The article was fascinating.

Laura's despondency lifted – just a little. Perhaps her father had been right. Maybe an accountancy qualification would be the way to go. She could be her own person, then. Earn her own money. It wouldn't matter if men never took an interest in her. There were none that she wanted anyway now the one that she did want utterly despised her. She might as well go along the career path and carve a life for herself that way. Why not? Well, she thought to herself Maths that's why not. I need to get good at it. For the first time in ages, she felt a little spark of enthusiasm as she came up with a plan.

"Is Dad coming home tonight" she asked her mother tentatively whilst they were drinking tea together one morning at breakfast. It was a tricky subject and could send her mother's mood either way. Laura hated asking knowing it could affect the atmosphere in the house for the whole day. But it was a good day, he was due home that night.

At dinner, she joined in the conversation around the weather (it was a long hot summer), the drought (due to the long hot summer) and the Prime Minister's inability to plan for a long hot summer that he couldn't have foreseen. As her father took a bite of ice-cream, she saw her chance to jump in and asked if he would coach her with maths.

"All of it?" he enquired incredulously, swallowing hastily.

"Not quite all of it – well most of it. Ok, all of it. I think I need to start from scratch with somebody who can work at my pace but I want to try to become an accountant".

Her father tried hard to keep the scepticism out of his face but Laura caught it. Her mother beamed hoping narcissistically that this meant he would spend less time 'away on business'.

Laura knew her father, John, was the financial director of a big national company and spent a lot of time away from home. She didn't know why or where he was when he wasn't there but it had always been the case and it affected her mother's moods so dramatically that they rarely touched on the subject.

After scraping the last of the ice-cream from his bowl, he considered something and looked up.

"Of course, I'll help you. But it will be the tough love way, I'm afraid. The only way to get through exams is to thoroughly understand your subject and to do that you will have to work at it. I am going to be a hard task master but one day you'll thank me for it".

Laura tried hard not to have second thoughts. She couldn't. She wanted to be independent and not wait for a man to be the reason whether her day was good or bad. She would work hard and she would make it.

The rest of the holidays, starting with the basics, she worked on her maths every morning. Sat at the dining room table surrounded by books, compasses, slide rules and protractors she hummed along to the tunes on Radio 1's roadshow. She stopped, temporarily, to listen to the 'Bits and Pieces' quiz when you had to guess the artist of 10 tunes played in short consecutive bursts then carried on with her school work. One day as she was shouting answers at the radio her mother observed wryly that if she was half as good at maths as she was at knowing pop tunes, she would go a long way!

In the afternoons she sun-bathed in the stifling heat, walked into town and browsed records in Woolworths with Jane and Sally or strolled across the brown dusty fields to the trickle which was no longer a river.

By the time September and the new term rolled around she felt more confident about maths. It was the only thing but it was a start, finally there was a tiny crack of light at the end of the long dark tunnel which she called her life. By the end of the month Laura had found something else to turn her life around and she was called Farrah. She starred in a US TV show which took the world by storm and Laura idolised her. Not that she met her, knew her or even came close to going to the USA but to Laura the actress was the epitome of good looks and style. Jaclyn was a true beauty and Kate was the brainy one. Both ladies had huge appeal but Farrah, with her girl next door looks, bright smile and blonde flicked hair was the one Laura wanted to be like. Along with half the female population.

She began a diet in earnest, bought curling tongs, persuading her mother to scald her mousy poker straight hair into soft temporary curls, and copied Farrah's stylish looks after spending a small fortune on clothes in Chelsea Girl. She determinedly did not change at school continuing to wear her hair in a pony tail and sensible lace up shoes. She skulked around the edge of the playground or scurried down corridors unless she was under the sharp-tongued protection of Jane and Sally. She avoided the cool crowd and Steve as much as she could. Not that she really needed to, she was old chip paper to them. At the beginning of term one or two of the glossy girls had glanced in her direction and away again as if they had seen nothing more interesting than a fly on a window pane.

By the time the school year had moved around to late spring and Laura had finished the year with more of a whimper than a wail she had recovered a little of her composure and had worked hard enough to be confident about her exams. Her heart, was still broken and her feelings smashed to a pulp but stifling them made her insides harden and she became good at hiding her emotional desert feigning empathy with anybody who required it, like a professional.

August 1977 was much the same as 1976 except it was nowhere near so hot and a good deal of it was spent waiting for what were ultimately excellent exam results. Laura changed her mind completely and stayed on at the school to do A Levels. The year thinned out significantly. She no longer had to loiter about in corridors and hide in the library at lunchtime as she had been doing. School got a bit easier to cope with because Steve Miles and the, as it turned out, brainless glossies left it.

Laura thought she might care about never seeing him again but it was easier than she thought. Not seeing him meant she could fool herself that somewhere out there he wasn't a mean-spirited bully. He would grow up and realise that he had lost the love of his life then come looking for her. The bit she didn't understand was why she still cared. She had seen him for what he was yet the feeling that he was the only man she would truly ever want remained. It was inexplicable. In the last year she had secretly watched him when she could. Standing at windows, she had seen him walk into school or play football at lunchtimes. He had a jaunty walk and an easy grin which he bestowed on anybody but her. Sometimes she saw him in the corridor talking to Lorraine Carter who was slim and pretty with long shiny blonde hair. A real-life Farrah. She would perch on a radiator and he would stand over her with his arm up the wall bracing himself, protective but not quite touching her, sexual tension hanging in the air. Laura skulked by and hoped they didn't see her. In one excruciating episode he sat on the desk in front of her for one of the exams and she had to look at the curls brushing his shirt collar and his strong tanned arms showing below the rolled back sleeves of his white school shirt for two hours. The physical desire for him was overwhelming. He acted as if she didn't exist.

Perversely, once he had gone, she felt a little less empty. Only Sally had stayed on so they hung around together in the 6th form common room listening to Blondie and the Police, on the large prehistoric wood panelled radio tuned to Radio 1, and gossiping. Pupils from other forms that they hadn't known well joined in and they became friends. Some lunchtimes were fun. Some days the emptiness receded a little.

Out of the blue Paul had asked her out. The girls had persuaded her to go to a local village disco. The hall was half full when they got there and the music was ramped up even though it was quite early. Coloured lights flashed up and down and around and around bouncing off the walls and the ceiling. They bought a bottle of coke each and stood sucking on their straws and chatting in the corner hoping that some more people would turn up. There were other groups clumped together, each set eyeing the other with something between interest and boredom. A boy with his head down and hands in the pockets of his baggy jeans disentangled himself from a bunch of kids in the opposite corner and shuffled around the edge of the empty dance floor towards them. Looking at all the girls at the same time, then at his feet, he said "Paul wants to know if you will go out with him?". "Which one of us?" asked Jane sharply. "You" he said and pointed to Laura. The girls went straight to the toilets for a talk. Laura was shaking.

"Paul who?" she asked querulously.

"Paul Webster" Jane supplied the information as if this should have meant something to Laura.

"And he is….?"

"Oh, come on" Sally joined in "he's in the year above, goes around with Johnny Brownly, and Pete Stewart".

Was there nothing that went on in the school that her friends didn't know? Sometimes she found it irritating and now was one of those times.

"I thought they had a reputation for having a different girlfriend every week?"

"Where did you hear that?" Jane was curious.

"From you, who do you think I heard it from? The Sun has got nothing on you two for spreading the gossip". Laura's voice dripped sarcasm which completely missed its mark when Jane said "Really? Oh, thank you". Laura rolled her eyes at herself in the mirror.

"So, are you going to meet him or not?" Sally was insistent "you can't keep the poor boy waiting for ever".

Why not, thought Laura, she didn't owe him anything. Just because he liked the look of her face or whatever it was it didn't mean she had some obligation towards him.

"He's not my type" she whined. How she could possibly tell? She had no idea because she didn't know him but it seemed like a good argument. It wasn't.

"Please don't tell me that your type is Steve Miles, Laura?" Sally hissed. "Hopefully this one won't treat you like shit".

Laura knew she was defeated. She couldn't tell her friends what she felt because they had really looked after her but expecting them to believe that she would never be interested in another man was pushing their immature friendship boundaries too far so she agreed to meet Paul.

Paul and Laura walked together out of the disco towards a playing field where the mist had risen from the grass making the place seem ethereal and ghostly. He was tall and skinny, with large lips and eyes slightly too close together and really not her type. Laura felt the emptiness descend on her again but battled to appear interested. She would have to disentangle herself from this, she knew. He was sweet and kind and asked questions about her. What street did she live in? What music did she like?

What was she going to do after school? He was a farm labourer but was going to join the Army in a month's time. She was mildly impressed. He had aspirations – she liked that. She started to shiver, it was a cold night, and she had only worn a cardigan. He took off his denim jacket and moved to put it around her shoulders but as he did so, drew her to him and bent to kiss her. She hesitated, then closed her eyes and let him do so. The kiss was soft and wet and intrusive and became physically overwhelming as he pressed himself to her. She didn't like it and wanted to fight to get away. This was not what she wanted, not who she wanted. A shout from Sally broke them apart. Her mother had come to pick them up and was waiting in the car park so Laura had to go. Paul asked to see her again and flustered she said yes. He took her phone number.

Sat in the back of the car on the way home with her head resting on the cold window glass she turned her feelings over in her head. Sally had wanted to know the finer details of what had happened but Laura didn't have much to tell. She had felt flattered that a boy had taken an interest in her but, if she was truthful, it just vaguely touched her ego. Maybe she would have felt differently if Paul had been somebody she had wanted to go out with. But he wasn't and it just left her feeling cold and empty.

A few days later her mother answered the house phone and with a quizzical note in her voice said there was a young man asking to speak to her. They agreed to meet on Friday night at the cinema to see Jaws 2. She hoped Jaws 2 was a little less papier-mache than Jaws 1 had been but concluded that it probably wouldn't matter, anyway.

Paul wore a clean white button-down shirt under a denim jacket with jeans. He had had a severe hair cut which made his slightly red nose look big. He smelt of Brut aftershave – his Dad's he confessed later. "You look nice" he had said. She had gone the whole – Farrah -hog. Hair carefully tonged into tumbling hair lacquered curls, flared FU's jeans, a checked shirt with a cream jumper thrown casually over her shoulders. This look took Farrah a lot of places. Looking in the mirror Laura realised that she had lost a bit of weight and the jeans fitted snugly.

The jumper completed her look but it was cold and she wished she could actually wear it.

They sat at the back of the quarter-full cinema which made her nervous. Her palms sweated and when Paul tried to take her hand, she pretended she needed to use her hanky. Discreetly she wiped them. She told herself to calm down and let him hold her hand. The film was awful, and it didn't take long for him to wind his arm across her shoulders then creep down to her breast. He started kissing her. At first small, quick dry ones then longer sloppier wetter ones. She began to feel uncomfortable and writhed around in the seat. He took this as encouragement and continued whispering in her ear and touching her chest. She did not enjoy it, in fact it revolted her but this was what was expected. She would have to get used to it.

At school she gained a small amount of respect. She had a boyfriend and people looked at her differently. In an attempt to bolster her reputation Sally had wasted no time in spreading the news and she began to be included in conversations that she hadn't been before. In truth, she wished she hadn't been. The talk was about love-bites and blow jobs and contraception and she felt out of her depth. She made excuses to get away citing homework and took refuge in a corner of the library. But part of her liked it, she liked the feeling of belonging to an exclusive club. Somebody desired her, that lumpy dumpy person with long straight hair she caught a reflection of as she walked along the glass lined corridor to class.

The bit she really liked was when Paul went away to Army training. She had the best of both worlds. She still had a boyfriend, one that was going to have a career, but she didn't have to put up with the mauling and groping and the attempts at cold sex that went with it. She grew a little. Her anxiety lessened. She ate a little more. Her mother was surprised "Thought you might be love-sick" she said.

Two weeks later it was all over. Paul was back. He couldn't cope with the training. He had found it too hard and failed the second serious test he had been given. He was going to be a farm labourer again. Life was good he could go back to going to the pub. Laura put the phone down on him and hid upstairs when he came to the door.

Chapter 8 – Twenty-five

Steven hired a moped and they toured around the Island stopping off at secluded coves. They lay on hired sun beds under umbrellas on the beach, wandered amongst the pine trees or paddled in the clear blue water hand in hand. She felt safe tucked behind his large shoulders, her hands clasped around his waist and the warm wind caressing her skin as they flew along.

Laura's arms and legs became lightly tanned although she was careful to shade her face. She dined on salad and drank water while Steven tucked into burgers and fish. Loud speakers relayed the likes of Wham's 'Club Tropicana' and Culture club into the hot evening air. Whilst drinking sangria and smoking cigarettes they chatted about life and his interests – mostly motorbikes of which she knew nothing. She struggled to engage him with her love books and foreign sub-titled films. Too intellectual for a dumb country boy he told her, both loving and feeling intimidated by her intelligence. She laughed not quite wanting to believe it. They shared a dry sense of humour.

In bed he was a surprisingly thoughtful lover. He marvelled at her soft skin, stroked her flat stomach and caressed her hair. He made her feel secure. One morning after they had woken up entwined in each other's arms she swung her legs out of the bed and whispered "I'm off for a run, you get some sleep". She smiled at him as he dozed with one arm under his head revealing dirty blonde underarm hair. Lazily opening one eye he said "Do you really need to? We're on holiday can't you give it a rest for a few days?".

Laura felt her heart quicken with stress. She did need to. She took on board calories and calories needed burning off especially as Steven's idea of a walk was half a mile along the beach front to the local taverna. Fat, fat, fat. That word had run through her brain on a loop since that fateful morning. She measured everything in terms of fat. Was she fat? Were they fat? Did that food have fat in it? How much fat? Was any fat good for you? She knew this was not healthy but could not turn the perpetual incessant sound track to her life off so she resolved to beat it in the only way she knew how. She would out-run it. Now, she had to deal with somebody else guessing her guilty secret and somehow head him off. She turned around with a false smile and tried a different tactic.

"If you don't want me to, then I won't" she said whilst bending down and appearing to unlace her trainers.

She held her breath hoping he wasn't going to play that game – trying to tell her what to do - because her exercise was one thing she was not going to compromise on. It was alright for him he had a washboard flat stomach despite his large frame but she had to work hard to get hers anywhere close.

He grinned. "Don't be daft – if you want to go then go. It's your holiday, too!" and he rolled over and closed his eyes. Sleepily he mumbled "To me it seems like you're obsessed but if you are its fine – it happens to the best of us".

Laura darted out of the room before he could change his mind and the day would be ruined with an atmosphere. He understood her and didn't mind her lifestyle choices. Relief pulsed through her. Obsessed, of course, she was obsessed what was he thinking?

Laura's lifestyle choice had happened as soon as she had left home. Her A levels had gone well and much to her surprise the University of Sheffield had accepted her on an Accounting and Management course. Her father was delighted, he told her on one of his increasingly infrequent evenings at home, and started throwing career ideas at her until she was sick of hearing them. Her mother was not – she would lose her 'raison d'etre'.

Before packing up and leaving home Jane had persuaded Laura to change her hairstyle. It will make you feel entirely different she had told her.

"I doubt it" Laura had been despondent. Her personal self-esteem still sailed merrily along somewhere near rock bottom and Jane was training to be a hair stylist not a psychologist!

Nevertheless, the fringed bob she sported afterwards swung seductively and glossily at her shoulders. It framed her face and took the edge off her too large nose. Jane tried to pluck her eyebrows but Laura resisted. "I don't want to look like a doll, thank you very much". Jane plucked the odd stray hair and the ones between her eyebrows and stood back with a triumphant 'there' proud of her work.

After almost physically detaching herself from her mother's apron strings It didn't take Laura long to work out that university life suited her very well. She found the first year in the halls of residence daunting but also lively with an energetic buzz. Intellectually she couldn't believe she had the necessary brains but nobody questioned her so she attended lectures and took on board as much as she could. Socially, there was always something going on and she could choose to join in or not. She didn't feel an outcast but she didn't feel she had to be involved either. She liked the independence and the ability to choose her own path but she found her social inadequacies hard to overcome. She took up jogging and found it gave her a sense of freedom and time to think. It was starting to become a 'thing' and there were a few clubs she could have joined to run with company but she preferred to do it alone. Away from her mother's starchy food offerings she researched then cooked herself healthy meals and did four hundred stomach crunches a day. After she had met Donna and Melanie, she also took up smoking and drinking.

Two weeks after arriving in Sheffield Donna had poked her head around Laura's open door with a packet of cigarettes and a pink Bic lighter in one hand and a bottle of Woodpecker in the other. "Do you want to come?" she said nodding her head towards the sunny afternoon outside. Laura could think of nothing better to do apart from read so nodded an acquiescence and went along. Donna introduced her to Melanie who was petite, blonde and universally popular it seemed. Donna was the reverse, larger framed with short brown hair, dangly earrings and a mannish dress sense. She and Melanie were an incongruous pair but they were generous with their friendship and included Laura without an inquisition which made her feel a sense of belonging and confidence she had never felt before. As they sprawled on the grass on that first meeting with a tinny transistor playing disco tunes by

Donna Summer and Rose Royce they discussed politics, the sexiness of John Travolta and whether Mick Jagger could dance. Donna offered Laura a cigarette and she took one in an attempt at sophistication then fooled nobody by coughing and spluttering through her first few inhalations. "First one of the day?" Melanie asked drily "First one of my life!" Laura had replied.

Thanks to Donna and Melanie, Laura had a social life. She was invited to parties and nights at the pub. Popping outside for a smoke created a camaraderie and from there, acquaintances who would nod at her as she made her way to lectures. Nods turned into greetings then longer chats. She made more friends. She revelled in the life and for the first time felt that she was the person she was meant to be.

One day she took all her clothes off and looked in the mirror again. Her legs and arms were an even colour. Her breasts were shapely and her stomach was flat and thanks to depilatory cream hair did not grow on any part of her body that it shouldn't. Her bottom had definition and her face was framed nicely by her expensively conditioned glossy hair. Blue eye-liner and an abundance of Boots No 17 mascara emphasised her eyes and her upper lip was plucked clean. When she smiled, she could almost deceive herself that inside she was as sorted as outside. Almost!

Whilst dancing to Tavares with Donna in a deafening disco one night she noticed a man at the bar looking in their direction. She wore her tight cream trousers and brown satin shirt. Her hair was a mass of bouncing curls that she had managed to achieve with curling tongs and half a can of hairspray. By the end of the night, she knew her hair would be flat to her skull but at that moment it looked good. She and Donna danced in duo complementing each other's moves. They were attracting attention and they knew it. Donna twirled past her ear and yelled "He's been staring at you all night". Laura was sure Donna was wrong but as she bobbed and turned in time with the beat, smiling at her companion she kept an eye on him. Donna was right he was watching her. It made her feel self-conscious suddenly and she abruptly stopped, tapped her friend's arm and pointed vaguely in the direction of the toilets. Donna nodded, eyes half closed, lost in the earthy tones of 'More than a

Woman', the disco ball twirling above her head sending shards of sparkling light onto her hair and the writhing mass of people surrounding her.

As Laura moved across the dance floor, skirting flailing arms and avoiding men with two left feet, her wrist was grabbed by somebody in the melee. She turned with an affronted look to find the stranger had materialised at her side. He pointed to the quiet bar unable to make himself heard above the blaring music and curious she followed him. She was flattered by the fact that out of that room of glamorous, slim alluring women he had chosen her. She fervently hoped he wasn't a pervert or a rapist as he led her up the steps.

Up close he was a young man. His looks were dark and swarthy which made him look older from a distance but in reality, he was around Laura's age. This reassured her. He couldn't be any more sophisticated than her, surely? He had black tousled hair that covered his ears and was slim hipped. His lips were thin, his nose fitted his face perfectly but his eyes were dark and unfathomable. He disguised this with a smile that warmed his features. His name was Marcus and he came from London and Laura realised that she had seen him before. He had been part of Melanie's entourage one night – friends of friends – he had told her later but it made her feel better. She put her safety fears to the back of her mind. Other people knew him, it was fine. He was a history student and made her laugh by telling her stories about his school days.

After the night of the disco, they had gone out on a real date, one where they could talk in normal voices and she could have straight hair and a lot less mascara. Marcus was easy company and she got into the habit of seeing him two or three times a week. They went for a walk or to the student bar where they hid in a corner and smoked. Until then she had been on a few dates, nothing serious. A couple she had slept with, others she had fought off. None of the sex had been very satisfying and left her feeling mauled afterwards. In those times she wished she hadn't grown up and could go back to being nine nor ten again when life's sordid little secrets hadn't affected her and she had been in love with ponies.

One evening Marcus asked if he could take her to see a film. She agreed, secretly hoping that it wasn't going to be a war documentary or horror. It turned out to be called "Emmanuelle". They had driven to the cinema although they could easily have taken a bus and on the way back, she found out why. Marcus took a detour out of the town to a dark country lane where he reversed into a field gateway. Before he had killed the engine, they were stripping off their clothes and having hot sweaty sex on the back seat of his car. Laura liked his face and his sense of humour but his thin body did not attract her. He didn't have that muscly back that spoke of kicking footballs into the penalty area or bowling a spin ball on a brown cricket pitch. She kept her eyes closed and imagined he was somebody else. Somebody she really wanted. But in that moment of sexual desperation, she both needed him and knew she didn't want him. They didn't speak afterwards, just dressed, slipped back into the front seats of the car and drove back towards the lights that got brighter and brighter as the city approached. When her friends asked what film they had seen she made out that it was something high-brow and intellectual.

This ritual carried on for four months and despite herself she enjoyed the weekly cinema visits. It was addictive, the pheromones running wild straight afterwards and only sated a while later. It was a great antidote to the law and quantitative measures lectures that challenged her brain on a daily basis.

One hot evening after they had a few drinks in the packed pub he came back to her room. She closed the door and slipped off her shoes as he told her a funny anecdote he had overheard. She walked seductively towards him slowly unbuttoning her shirt as she did so but he shook his head and said quietly "Not tonight Laura". She was confused he had been attentive all night, hadn't given her any indication that anything was wrong. Was he tired? She enquired. No, he said, he just wasn't in the mood and he left.

She understood. It didn't have to be spelt out in front of an audience this time. She'd been rejected and it hurt but she was getting used to it. It's what men did. Months later she realised she missed the porn more than him.

Chapter 9 – Twenty-five

After two years at University Laura worked at a placement for a year. Her father found her an accountancy firm specialising in auditing 50 miles from where she grew up. Close enough to home but too far to commute every day, much to her relief.

The business took over floors six and seven of a large office block. There were endless amounts of offices as well as large open spaces filled with desks. Plants on every corner and data input clerks clattering on keyboards. Besuited men and women with big hair and even larger shoulder pads walked in and out of meeting rooms returning to their desks to stare earnestly at large box-like monitors, scribble things on pads and shout loudly across desks at each other. Telephones rang like an out of tune orchestra. As one was picked up and answered another started its insistent demand for attention. There was a buzz of activity from early morning until late into the evening. Mrs Thatcher's country was thriving and so in turn was the accountancy sector.

In the beginning Laura found it hard to believe that she belonged in this world and grappled with the workload and long hours. She tried to imagine her father in his crisp white shirt and pin-striped suit walking corridors like these, giving instructions and meeting important clients. She found that it was easy – he was made for it.

After two months she had settled in and started to feel that it would be a job she could enjoy. The smartly dressed strangers that intimidated her turned into real people with lives and families. Some even had time for a life away from the office although not many. The office banter was jocular and inclusive and also often highly sexist but she rebuffed any remarks aimed at her with a speedy and witty retort. She quickly learnt to have one at the ready and it gained her respect amongst her colleagues. She also learnt that self-protection was the only protection and she was becoming an expert at that.

One evening she was invited along to the local pub to say goodbye to a colleague who was leaving to have a baby. She had only ever exchanged pleasantries with the woman but had nothing better to do and she justified to herself that there was no law against anybody going to the pub for a drink. Despite the salubrious surroundings, the pub was a little ramshackle with poky rooms and small windows leaving the bar areas dark in the summer and cosy in the winter. It was a relic of a bygone age when it had sat on the edge of a river whilst barges floated past and there were only a few buildings nearby. Now it was surrounded by glass and chrome and it looked incongruous. None of this appeared to affect its popularity and the place was packed. After a couple of Martini and lemonades Laura felt hot in the busy bar and after waving a cigarette packet and gesturing to her colleagues went into the back garden for a smoke. It was bike night and the garden and car park were also packed although mercifully the air was vast above her head and a whole lot cooler. It smelt of two-stroke petrol, drains and petunia oil. She leaned against a wall, one leg bent at the knee, lit a cigarette and with a long drag closed her eyes. She felt rather than heard somebody stand beside her and say "I don't suppose I could cadge one, could I? I've run out". The voice was friendly. Still with her eyes closed immersed in the sensation of the first nicotine hit from the cigarette Laura held out the gold packet and lighter then opened her eyes and looked at the speaker. He had long dirty blonde hair, pale blue eyes and a smile that showed even white surprisingly unstained teeth. He was around 5'10" with strong shoulders and arms and wore a black leather jacket and stained jeans. He gazed at the gold packet and said laconically "I'm more of a Marlboro man myself". Laura sized him up and down and waspishly said "No, you are really not!".

His name was Steven. Of course, it is, Laura had thought irrationally at the time. Just as she had started to get a life and stand on her own two feet something had to come along to put her head right back to where all her anxieties and insecurities lived.

"Everybody calls me Steve" he had told her. Laura did not. He had asked her out that night and unable to resist his smile Laura had said yes.

Steven had turned up in a car. A borrowed one he had told her afterwards but it was designed to impress and it worked. He had scrubbed up well. Hair combed, newly shaven, clean jeans and a light blue cotton shirt which accentuated his eyes, unwittingly she was sure because vanity did not appear to be one of his traits. They went to a night club in a nearby town to watch a band that Laura would never normally have thought of listening to. Steven told her a couple of anecdotes about previous gigs and the friend of a friend who knew the drummer's sister. Despite herself Laura had fun. She wasn't going to love him or marry him but in the absence of the one and only person she did want he was a good second best. He had kissed her chastely at the end of that date and asked if he could see her again. She had read this as old fashioned and chivalrous and liked it. She didn't feel that her private world of self-deprecation and deprivation would be threatened by him so she agreed. He wasn't one for long intimate chats in cosy corners but preferred being out and about doing something and he could always come up with something to do. On their fifth date he turned up with a grey back pack containing a black, second hand but beautifully smelling leather jacket and a red and white helmet over his arm. From that night on she became a biker chick. Because of his motorbike riding and a few minor scrapes with the police, she found out that he had a bit of a bad boy reputation and she found it thrilling. Nobody that edgy had ever taken an interest in her. He was an oddball – no doubt about that - but a likeable one. They saw each other four or five nights a week. Although his friends referred to Laura as Steve's girlfriend, Steven's girlfriend she corrected in her head, it wasn't an intimate relationship. They had sex which was in Laura's view better than she had expected but they didn't make future plans. She didn't want to and he never brought it up. Steven seemed happy to live in the moment and Laura had no desire for an intense relationship because nice as he was, he wasn't the one, that had been decided 10 years before. For his part, Steven wanted to spend time with his mates discussing motorbike riders she had never heard of and the merits of a good exhaust system so it suited them both.

After a successful year and the offer of a job in the future if required Laura returned to university and as she did at school decided to make her last year count. She worked hard but found herself the centre of attention at lunchtime get togethers because of her maverick boyfriend. It gave her the same feeling of belonging that she had felt at school for those few days before Paul returned from his big career opportunity and pulled the rug from under her feet. In truth, Steven was no longer really her boyfriend. They hadn't made any promises of devotion to each other, not even ones of monogamy but had agreed to go their separate ways, stay in touch and see what happened. Laura had enjoyed the ride, both literally and metaphorically, but moved on with her life in a way that surprised even herself. He visited her once on a dry cold day in early December when they walked down to Castlegate and looked at the slate grey waters of the River Don rippling in the fast-moving breeze. Their conversation was stilted and not easy and free-flowing as it had been back in the summer. Away from his comfort zone Steven resorted to taciturnity and she had found it exhausting thinking of something to say. He didn't visit again.

After graduation Laura and Melanie decided to take a long holiday in France. Melanie had had enough of the attentions of men for a while and they decided that they got on well enough to attempt the trip. The obvious starting point was Paris where they wandered along the Champs Elysees and down the elegant tree lined streets. Laura let Melanie ascend the Eiffel Tower on her own whilst she stayed below avoiding the street sellers, waving ridiculously when she thought her friend had reached the top. After the capital they drove the battered open top sports car, they had pooled together to hire for the trip down country through Limoges, Toulouse and past the magnificent Carcassonne until they reached Perpignan. There they stayed in a caravan and spent most days on the beach and swimming in the crystal blue waters of the Mediterranean. The bright blue sky, terracotta rooves, white washed walls and vermilion flowers gave Laura the feeling of joyous freedom.

Led face down on the sun bed with her hands raking the sand backwards and forwards Melanie asked one day "Were you in love with him?". From behind her sunglasses Laura opened her eyes suddenly. She had been thinking about Steve Miles and it was as if Melanie had just looked into her soul. "With whom?" She had wanted to say, with who, but remembered not to just in time. "Marcus?" said

Melanie. Marcus, thought Laura, where the hell had that come from?

When they had decided on their trip Laura had called her mother and told her of the plan. She tried to time it so that she could extricate herself quickly from the conversation if she needed to but her mother was on good form. She had, apparently, recently taken up yoga and tennis and had a new lease of life. She had recovered from empty nest syndrome and made a fresh start. Laura was glad. Her mother sounded enthusiastic about the holiday and requested interesting postcards which she could show to her friends. Just before the call ended, her mother clearly having had an extrication plan of her own said "Jane has asked if you will call her – she has news".

Laura was not sure she wanted to hear Jane's news. It could be quite parochial and she often found her mind drifting whilst the tinny voice droned on about her relationship with her fiance, Terry who was renovating a house they had bought and her father's arthritis. Dutifully she made the call. That day her friend had gossip.

"Guess who got married?"

Laura's curdled stomach did not share the excitement in her friend's voice.

"No idea, who?" She asked hoping her voice sounded light.

"Steve Miles and Lorraine Carter!" Jane sounded triumphant as if she was Cilla Black and had personally introduced the couple on Blind Date. Do you remember him? It was a big white wedding in the Abbey then a reception at the hotel next door. We went to the evening do being as Lorraine's mum is Terry's mum's cousin. The food was….". Laura zoned out. She felt something ice cold grip her heart and her head span. Did she remember him? Had her friend lost her mind after years of cutting hair and tweezing eyebrows? How would she ever forget him? Laura's lack of response didn't register with her friend and she rattled on until she ran out of details then after a yell, a crash and a lot of swearing in the background hurriedly rang off. Laura's hands shook. What was she expecting? That his life hadn't carried on? That other women wouldn't find him attractive? That he would realise she was the one for him? She was such a fool! Why did she care?

This was a man that had publicly humiliated her, trodden her self-esteem into the ground, made her previously happy life irrevocably miserable and she still couldn't get him out of her head. He had clearly sent her mad, too!

"Not a chance" said Laura, back in the present and replying to Melanie's question about Marcus and rolled over to bake the front half of her body. She really needed it to match her back otherwise she would look like one of those Praline chocolates from the Milk Tray box. She didn't want to discuss her love life with Melanie who had many good qualities but her idea of discretion was not to tell the man at the petrol station.

After Marcus's rejection Laura shut up emotional shop. She didn't feel that she deserved to be treated like that by either him or anybody else and she wasn't going to let it happen again. Lying in bed at night, sleep a distant memory, she analysed her feelings delving deeper and deeper until she realised that if she stopped caring about anybody or anything then there would be nothing left to hurt her. Probably not the healthiest outlook on life but who was she reporting to? People could do what they liked but she wasn't going to be made to care. She didn't understand romance, it seemed to be a euphemistic word for good times which ended in misery and upset.   She put up mental barriers like little armadillo scales. Protection she liked to think, from the world. She learnt how to act the part and did it well. After so many years of feeling that she was a round peg in a square hole and didn't really belong anywhere it liberated her. There was only one person that had the ability to get through that shield and he was a prick. A married prick!

Was there a way of explaining all of that to Melanie? She didn't think so

Laura was sure he would have looked handsome in a dark grey suit with a pink carnation in his button hole. His blonde hair curling gently over the edge of his white shirt. His mouth that could say such vile things would have been curved upwards in a smile as he said the words "I, do" to the pretty blonde prom queen that he had married. The thoughts started to hurt. She picked up her book. She put down her book. She had an argument in her head with her newly formed younger self. Did you think you were going to marry him? Asked the 25-year-old Laura. No, lied the 15-year-old Laura unconvincingly. You did! Jeered the 25-year-old Laura. You are so naïve. I'm 15, said the 15-year- old Laura. Of course, I am naïve but what do you do when you find the love of your life at my age and he rejects you? How are you supposed to get through the rest of your life? You stop being so pathetic and grow up replied the 25-year-old Laura unkindly.

Chapter 10 – Twenty-five

One nano-second after Steve Miles had uttered those fateful life-changing words to Laura, he had forgotten about them. Up until then he had been consumed with a burning fury. Who did this girl think she was? She had made him the laughing stock of his class and he barely knew her. He chatted to lots of people, was friendly, was well- liked, had a certain standing in the school cool hierarchy. He liked the feeling and at 15 was breezing through life without a care for anybody. He really could not be bothered with silly little fat girls mooning over him. But wherever he went she seemed to be there. First of all, he tried ignoring her but she still hung around then he tried to convey his lack of interest by blanking her or staring back at her with hard cold eyes across the chemistry classroom but she hadn't got the message. It would just have to be a short sharp shock, like Lorraine suggested. The girl had been mortified as he succinctly told her what he thought of her but he barely noticed. The cool girls laughed smugly knowing they were on the right side of the social divide and the boys jeered, well, Al didn't but the rest did. Steve had no idea what was the matter with him but that thought was even more fleeting than the first one. The group ran off down the corridor hooting and hollering in a rush to get on with the rest of their life.

After his O levels Steve hadn't really known what he was going to do. He was half- hearted about A levels but as luck would have it there had been a vacancy in a high street bank as a junior teller so he applied and got the job. Al, went to technical college to become a plumber and he knew he didn't want to do that. He liked working with figures and if he played his cards right there was a career ahead of him.

It hadn't taken a lot of courage to move on to kissing Lorraine good night and then on to a bit more than that. She was very pretty, something he could recognise in girls, and he knew a lot of men in the town envied him. She could also be vacuous but what did he care? They didn't have deep conversations about politics, the FTSE 100 or the chances of England winning the world cup. Humour wasn't her thing he noted early on and witticisms sailed so far over her head that had they been a missile the 7.20 pm flight from London to New York would have crashed and burned. He worked, studied for banking exams, played football at weekends and dated Lorraine. Lorraine committed herself to always looking good, having perfect nails and wearing fashionable clothes. She wanted to be a hairdresser and got an apprenticeship in a town centre salon. They made a handsome couple.

When he was 21, two things happened. His mother died of breast cancer and he nearly went off the rails. He managed to hold it together at work but spent more and more evenings at the pub. Lorraine was not as comforting as she might have been and preferred to go to bed for her beauty sleep rather than listen to his woes so he found solace in the arms of a girl called Mandy who always seemed to be at the bar at the right time. A small piece of gossip that Lorraine chose to believe got back to her and they split up for three years.

Mandy had married young to a long-distance lorry driver who went by the charming name of Mental Micky. Not for no good reason, it turned out. His hard man reputation was well known. Mandy was a nice girl and a had a way of listening when it was required and joining in with the fun when that was required. They had sex against the back wall of the pub a few times and she persuaded him to turn his grief into something useful. The first thing was to pay more attention to his father who was also suffering whilst having to look after Steve's younger sibling. The second was to start running marathons and raise money for breast cancer charities. By the time Steve got back together with Lorraine after swearing undying devotion and they married he was regarded as an all-round good guy.

After the initial new romance happiness had waned a little Lorraine worried that she and Steve might split up again so took things into her own hands and forgot to take the pill for a few weeks. Consequently, their engagement and marriage came along rather quicker than Steve would have liked. He had a last fling with Mandy in the early hours of his wedding morning after he had drunk far too much on his stag night, the previous evening, then squared his shoulders for married life.

The 13th century Abbey looked magnificent against a sapphire blue cloudless sky and he felt like a film star as he waved to the many well-wishers in the grounds. His last marathon had raised over £10,000 and he had appeared in the local paper, looking sweaty and charitably smug. He had done his bit. The townsfolk were very appreciative and showed it. Shafts of sunlight dappled the worn pastel-coloured tiles on the floor, the lavish flower displays perfumed the interior and the buzz of excited chatter from the smartly dressed guests greeted him as he walked down the aisle to take his place with Al in the right-hand front pew facing the altar. His last-minute jitters were gone and wedded bliss awaited.

The vicar gave an uplifting sign with his hands, the congregation got to their feet and the organ started up with Wagner's wedding march. Steve hadn't known it was written by Wagner until Al told him. He was surprised that Al knew. Lorraine appeared at his left arm, with a veil over her face and looking more like a meringue that Steve would have liked but he reassured her that she looked beautiful and she rewarded him with sparkling 'come hither' eyes and a large smile.

Forty-five minutes later, to the sound of the church bells, Mr and Mrs Steve Miles walked back down the aisle and emerged blinking into the sunlight. The photographer's shutters flashed and a reporter from the local rag asked for a comment from the bride on securing such a heroic husband. She was delighted and madly in love with him, she said.

At the reception Lorraine spent an inordinate amount of time discussing her dress, nails, flowers, underwear, hair, veil and vertiginously high ivory satin shoes with her girlfriends and interested female family members. Steve nearly had a heart attack when Al brought up the stag night in the Best Man's speech but he turned it into a risqué joke about something that hadn't really happened and he breathed easy again.

After the cake had been cut and Steve's tie knot had started to descend towards his navel, he overheard snatches of a conversation between Al and Terry Atkins.

"She got a 2:1"

"Sheffield, I think"

" …..lost two stone …."

"working in accounts or something in the city"

"Don't know"

Steve had no idea who they were talking about and lost interest as Lorraine glided up to him looking like a Disney princess.

At 27, two years later, with a toddler screaming for three hours every night and his wife looking more like one of the ugly sister's than Cinderella, Steve was not so sure that marriage was for him.

Chapter 11 – Thirty-five   1996

Laura moved close to the mirror so that one eye was bigger than the other and carefully applied blue eyeliner along the lower edge of her left eye then along the rim. She leant back and checked to see that it looked even then applied it to her right eye.

She added dark blue eyeshadow and a lot of mascara.

Jane was throwing a 35th birthday party and Laura and Steven had been invited. Laura knew that Steven would not want to go and if she was truthful neither did, she.

"Why are you having a 35th party?" she had asked the tinny voice.

"Because I was hugely pregnant when it was my 30th and missed out on having one. So, I want a party and I thought I would be different. Anyway, it will be fun – you'll enjoy it"

Laura highly doubted it. She also tried to suppress the thought that it would be the first time in her life that Jane had been different but it just maliciously squeezed in to one of her brain cells. Steven kicked up a fuss as she knew he would.

"When is it?" he had eventually enquired after Laura had dropped subtle then unsubtle hints about it for a couple of weeks.

"This Saturday"

"Busy" he said and went out to his garage. That usually meant he would go but not without moaning for days beforehand until he got there then he would transform into St Gregarious of Funsville and abandon her for the best part of the evening.

Laura sometimes struggled to align the man she was married to now with the man she had started going out with. She didn't imagine she was the first woman to have to do that.

After her tour of France with Melanie, Laura's father had put a word in for her with an accountancy firm that specialised in auditing in the nearby city. Unsurprisingly she was asked to go in for an interview. The country was in recession and after several rejections Laura was glad of the intervention. She had come back home to live after university and in the evenings watched Dynasty and Moonlighting with her newly emancipated mother.

Laura dressed carefully in a black skirt suit and high-heeled shoes for the interview and took a train to the city. The offices were on the 5th floor of a glass fronted building 10 minutes from the train station. Perched on the edge of a powder blue sofa in the reception area she waited to be called in. There was competition in the form of an earnest looking young man wearing glasses who kept looking at her legs.

The interview was conducted by a balding besuited middle-aged man in his forties. He looked like an accountant, Laura thought, pin stripes and a boring tie. Her credentials seemed fine, her lack of experience not too irksome, her father was regularly seen at the club, apparently, and his wife was looking forward to seeing her charming mother at the riding stables. It took Laura a minute to cotton on then she blanched and the man realised he had said something wrong.

She didn't get an offer.

Fortunately, two weeks later, she did. The job was in a similar building in a similar location and she got it on her own merits although the interviewer clearly recognised the surname but did not acknowledge it. She enjoyed the work, it was varied and meant working away from the office a few days a month. She was organised and applied neatness and good presentation skills to everything she did and it pleased her bosses. She won promotion after a year.

One her way back from the station one evening, her black high-heeled court shoes clicking on the pavement as she walked a roaring noise came up behind her. She didn't look around. She had learnt not to. Lone men slowed their cars to take a look, or hard-hat wearing workers from building sites would wolf whistle – it was partly flattering and partly disconcerting. She resolved to stare straight ahead.

A motorbike pulled up just in front of her, and the noise stopped. A man took off his helmet. She recognised him. It was Steven. He was riding a different motorbike than last time he told her afterwards. She wouldn't have known. His hair was shorter and in a style that suited him and he wore a checked shirt underneath his leather jacket. Like her he had quit smoking. Funny, she had said, because now you do look like the Marlboro man!

Laura enjoyed being with Steven again. She liked the contrast. City-smart accountant by day, biker chic by night. Once again, her reputation gained a dangerous edge and it thrilled her. They dated for 9 months seeing each other four or five times a week. Laura was introduced to a lot of his biker friends and they went on long pointless rides to cafes in the middle of nowhere for a cup of coffee. When Laura asked why they did that, Steven said it was so that they had somewhere to go. Laura introduced him to her friends and partners. The bike broke the ice with the men and before long they were his friends, too. He was a man's man.

One day when they were stopped at traffic lights, the engine idling noisily beneath them he opened his visor, turned his head and shouted something. From within her navy-blue padded helmet, Laura didn't hear a thing but nodded in agreement. Clinging on to his waist and catching the familiar aroma of leather and Denim aftershave she was sure it would be fine.

Four months later they were married. The week-long Majorcan holiday had been a success even if it had been in a previous lifetime so 30-odd years would be a doddle. Laura was swept along, her career was going well, she was married to a fun entertaining man. Perhaps life would be ok, tentatively the Armadillo shields stood down. Her confidence in her looks and abilities at an all-time high. She had fought and overcome the years of demons that those three, viciously spoken, little words had brought her. She barely thought of Steve Miles although a tiny what-if thought niggled away at the back of her brain when she gave it a chance too. As she grew older, she had no idea why. She had been a young foolish school girl obsessed with an immature boy, she told herself but maybe it was because he was the first one that had ever been nice to her. He had given her a feeling of intimate togetherness that she had never been able to forget or create with anybody else. She had liked that feeling and strove for it again. It was the measure she used for her relationships and in the end settled for what was a close as she knew she was ever going to get.

St Gregarious (Laura's private nickname for Steven's alter ego) accompanied them on holiday and stayed for a few weeks in their new home until one day he was gone. Whether it was sudden or gradual Laura was never able to work out but life changed.

Laura looked at the clock. Steven was playing his usual game. She put a dressing gown on over her underwear and padded down the garden to the garage in an old pair of trainers she kept by the door. The light was on and the radio was playing but she couldn't see anybody. She called out. Steven was lying on the floor on the other side of the motor bike squinting up at its underside with a torch between his teeth.

"Are you nearly done?" she asked trying not to make it sound like an accusation.

"What's the time?"

"7.30. We are supposed to be there by 8. They're going to do food first, then the cake then dancing"

Steven remained unmoved but sighed deeply. "Do I really have to go?"

"Yes" She turned on her heel and stalked back to the house.

Had he been so self-contained and laconic when they were going out? She didn't remember him being so – perhaps she had talked enough for two. They had spent a lot of time with his friends and they hadn't lived together so she wasn't sure. His demeanour was a series of nuances which she tried to read. In his case she had been a slow reader. His mother hadn't been much help when Laura had asked her if he had changed. No, she said, with Steven what you see is what you get. What was that supposed to mean? Was this her fault? Was this the effect she had on people or just men? Did he know that somehow, he was second best in her eyes – and she had got married in the heat of the moment because she was never going to get what she did want? She doubted all of that. More likely he hadn't changed at all she had just seen in him what she wanted and not seen the bits she didn't. Wasn't that the case in most marriages and didn't it work both ways? Probably. She should be thankful he wasn't a womaniser, a drinker or a gambler but he wasn't a companion either!

His laissez-faire attitude in Majorca had convinced her that he understood her, he got what she was about and he didn't mind. At the time she was amazed at his mature attitude and it had been one of the things that attracted her to him but he had shown no signs of such insight since. She threw herself into being the perfect everything, wife, mother of their twins and employee. Her frailties and anxieties hidden in plain sight on a daily basis. He was oblivious to it all. She once asked him during a bout of extremely low self-esteem if he thought she was pretty. He didn't reassure her – just said that he hadn't married her for her looks. Then what for? She had cried plaintively. He hadn't answered but, facial expression impassive, had turned on his heel and walked to the garage.

Laura and Steven arrived late for the party. Steven had showered and changed and looked good in a black shirt and jeans. Marlboro man meets St Gregarious. On the way they chatted about the twins (5 years old and safely tucked up in bed at

Steven's mothers house) an item Laura had seen on the news and whether to change the curtains in their bedroom. An ordinary married couple. They didn't row much. Steven was rarely nasty or unkind to her even when he was doing something, he didn't want to do but sometimes his lack of emotion annoyed her more. She felt superfluous, nothing derailed him from the introverted life that he led.

The hall was packed. The lights were up and guests were milling around carrying paper plates full of precariously balanced sausage rolls, egg sandwiches and crisps trying to also manage drinks in varying states of emptiness or fullness depending on how you viewed glasses. A banner above the disco proclaimed "Happy birthday lovely Jane". The empty dance floor had tables crammed around the edge like sunbathers on a beach in Benidorm perched on the edge of the sea. Groups of people were sat at them tucking into the food. The DJ had left the decks playing quietly as a background to the noisy buzz of chat and laughter. Who knew Jane was so popular? thought Laura, they probably wouldn't have been missed if they hadn't turned up after all.

"Laura, Steven! I am so pleased to see you both – I was getting worried – thought you might not be coming" Jane, in a low-cut red dress that framed her ample bosom rushed over, arms out stretched, as soon as she saw them.

"We would never do that to you" Steven lied, effortlessly charming, and kissed her on the cheek. "You look gorgeous". Jane preened and threw Laura a 'lucky you' look. Oh yes, Laura thought sardonically 'lucky me!'.

"Happy birthday, Jane" Laura said out loud. "We've got you a little something – where shall I put it?" Jane, gave the 'you shouldn't have' protest and pointed out a table which was stacked with presents and cards, then cried out to another couple of latecomers and went over to greet them. Laura made her way to the table as Steven moved towards the bar giving the 'getting a drink' hand gesture. She nodded and knew that would be the last she would see of him for a while.

A group of men stood by the table of presents laughing raucously. Laura excused herself and asked to be let through. One man slightly turned his head and Laura's stomach clenched and flipped. The curls on his shirt collar had barely changed in twenty years. Her heart pounded and she felt heat radiate through her body. She wanted to be anywhere else in the world apart from there. In a split second she felt inadequate, poorly dressed, over weight and completely unattractive.

She just about made it to the toilet cubicle in time. It was an anxiety attack, she had never had one, but knew that she was having one then. She put the toilet seat down and felt her heart hammering as she sat on it. Sweat poured uncomfortably into her fitted dress and through her tights. She looked at her hands and they were trembling; her breath was coming in short bursts. She needed a cigarette. As she bent over her knees to combat the nausea her hair fell forwards creating a curtain around her face and she closed her eyes. Images of jeering youngsters swam in front of them. Her Armadillo shield had forsaken her. She searched for it but it was gone. Violent emotion – this was it? This was the only thing that caused her to have violent emotion? She couldn't identify love, apart from maternal (so very different) or hate, even. She could do indifference professionally. But fear – fear made her senses scream. Fear of what? Failure, humiliation, rejection – all of those things. She had identified them – admitted them to herself. It felt the same as when she understood she had an eating disorder. Steven had nailed it yet it took her a long time to do the same. She called it her lifestyle choice but her extreme dieting, denying herself food, treating it as a reward for finishing a task and her obsessive need to exercise were not healthy. Was she damaged goods – was this why Steven withdrew from her? Was it why she had to pretend to everybody that the marriage was a great success? Lucky Laura – kids, husband, career all sorted. Of course, it was. If she failed at something, she had to work at it and then do it better than everybody else.

Laura opened her eyes and stared at the dirty floor. The tiles had probably been beige or grey years ago when they had been laid. Who had thought those colours would be a good idea in a public toilet? The dirt-filled cracks in the tiles made her feel sordid and she lifted her head to stare at the notice on the back of the door. 'Please leave this toilet in a state fit for others' it said. She found this amusing. She would have to get herself into a state that was fit for others and go back to the party. The bathroom door creaked as it opened and Laura heard the clicking of heels as somebody else came into the room. The door of the next-door cubicle slammed and she heard the noise of trickling water. She stood up and flushed the toilet to make it look as if she had used it and pulled the bolt back.

At the sink she washed her hands slowly then combed her hair back into shape and checked it in the mirror. The toilet flushed in the other cubicle and the door opened. She didn't look up but rummaged in her bag for her lip gloss then looked into the mirror to apply it. Sally was stood gazing into the mirror at her reflection. "You have no idea, at all, how attractive you are do you?" she said.

When Laura emerged from the toilet the lights had been dimmed and the decibel level had raised by a few hundred of whatever they were measured by. It was difficult to see who was who and she couldn't find anybody to aim for so decided to go outside and see if she could cadge a cigarette from one of the men who were bound to be out there getting away from watching their wives dance around their handbags.

The first drag of the cigarette felt good, it rolled like a wave through her body and she felt a relaxation that only nicotine can provide. She also knew it was only temporary but she made the most of the second and third drags, too.

"Laura Coombs?" a man enquired.

Lauran silently cursed. She didn't want to talk she just wanted to be left alone – was that too much to ask?

"I was, Laura Knowles, now"

It was Al. She didn't want to talk but also didn't want to be rude.

"Social smoker are you or the full-on 20-a-day kind of girl?" He was trying to be nice but Laura did not want to talk to him. He had been one of the sycophants on that far-away morning and she hadn't forgotten.

"Neither – I just occasionally smoke at parties – which I rarely go to" she qualified although had no idea why she felt the need.

"I hear you've done well for yourself – good job, nice house, nice car"

Laura inwardly smiled at the contrast between a man's view of achievement and a woman's and how things looked so different from the outside looking in.

"Nothing the matter with the grapevine, I'm pleased to hear" she said rather too sarcastically. She wasn't trying to be unpleasant – sometimes her thoughts and her voice just forgot which was which. Somewhere around her late twenties when life had dealt her more blows in varying degrees of severity and the cruelty, she had felt on that school morning was still too painful to dwell on, her inner voice had taken an edge of cynicism to it. As she moved into her thirties it became more intense and brought along a big dose of black humour. Life she realised, was not full of joyous moments of happiness and love but an endurance test full of large and small potholes some big enough to swallow you and others just there to trip you up especially if just for one minute you believed that there was a crock of gold at the end of the rainbow. Life, she decided, wore big-hob nailed boots and did as much kicking with them as it could and this was her way of dealing with it.

Laura finished her cigarette, blew smoke into the cold air and threw the butt down, grinding it out with the toe of her shoe before turning to walk back into the party. As she did Al said, admiringly, "You've certainly changed".

Calmer now she turned, smiled and replied. "Yes, I have".

The dance floor was crowded as she pushed her way through the room looking for Steven. She found him deep in conversation with Terry, both of them propped against the bar. Their heads were bent together so they could hear what the other was saying. Steven looked up and smiled at Laura as she approached then held his arms apart and made a throttle movement with one hand. They were talking about bikes. She knew they would be. Catching his eye again she pointed towards the dance floor and he nodded then pointed to his watch and showed her one finger. She had an hour to dance herself into oblivion.

'Don't you want me' by Human League was just starting and the writhing body mass doubled in size. The room vibrated with the base line of the music. The lights had been turned off after the food and the coloured ones from the disco flashed and moved jerkily around the room. Everybody shouted the chorus at the same time, laughing as they did so. It was hot and sticky and the lights disoriented the walls. The DJ read the room and kept the crowd pleasers going mercilessly. It got hotter and Laura wished she hadn't worn tights. As the bodies ebbed and flowed, she became aware of dancing next to a short blonde woman who wore a tight white dress which emphasised the rolls of fat around her waist. Her hair was cut into the same bobbed style as Laura's. The woman seemed to be in a world of her own so they danced side by side oblivious to each other but in that moment bonded by the feeling of freedom.

As the music finally calmed and Lionel Ritchie replaced Soft Cell, Laura turned to look for her husband. She couldn't see him but instead saw a man on the edge of the floor staring in her direction. The cold blue eyes were unmistakeable.

Chapter 12 – Thirty-five

On the Friday night before the party Steve had arrived home from work at the usual time to find his sausages and mash tea in the microwave looking like something even the dog wouldn't eat. Lorraine was lolled in a chair in the living room watching a sit-com on the television. She wore jeans, a stained and faded sweatshirt and dull grey cardigan that had seen better days. On her feet were well worn slippers and, on her face, not a scrap of make-up. Her hair was scraped up into a tatty ponytail and she was eating Maltesers out of their red cardboard box. Upstairs, to a backdrop of heavy drumbeats and music that he didn't recognise, his two children were squabbling loudly.

He poked his head around the living room door and greeted his wife.

"Hi, are you ok?"

"Yep" Lorraine didn't take her eyes from the screen. A scream could be heard from upstairs then a door slammed. The music was turned up a couple of notches.

"Is there any tea?" He was half hoping that the plate he had seen and tried to ignore wasn't for him.

"Yes" she looked at him now surprise in her voice "I did you some sausages and mash the same as we had. Give it a couple of minutes in the microwave and it'll be fine." She didn't move.

Steve thought it would take more than two minutes for that meal ever to be fine and contemplated upsetting Lorraine by chucking it in the bin and walking down the chippie. He refrained although his patience was on the edge.

Leaning against the kitchen counter with his sleeves rolled up, top two buttons of his shirt open and his tie knot half-way down his chest he watched the unappetising meal whirl around and around inside the lighted little box. He had no idea, now, why he had looked forward to Friday evening so much.

Steve did as little as he could get away with at the bank but still managed to work his way up the ladder by being in the right place at the right time. He liked the work providing it wasn't too hard and realised early on that the way to avoid getting his hands dirty was to get promotion and move away from day-to-day tasks as fast as possible. Therefore for a few years he worked harder than he would have liked but he looked on it as a necessary evil and as soon as he was able, he let his foot off the pedal. His plan worked very nicely for a few years. He offset his laziness by applying schoolboy charm to his female colleagues and buddying up with his male ones. It was a successful ploy and he was well liked.

When he was 32 things started to change in the banking sector and he knew that he would have to adapt or lose his generous pay check. Reluctantly he studied and took the necessary exams to keep himself ahead of the game and more importantly on the same standing as a lot of the new bright young interns flooding through the large glass and chrome doors eyeing his office with undisguised envy. He not only managed to stay ahead of the game but was offered promotion. This time it was a big one but there was a catch the job was in another city. The money was more than he ever expected to earn in his life and there was the chance of a divisional managership in the future. He rushed home to Lorraine full of excitement. He had made it, but they would need to move because it was a long commute. It would do them all good to get away from their hometown and start afresh. There were so many opportunities in the city. The words tumbled out.

"Opportunities to do what?" Lorraine had asked, flatly, with her back to him stirring Bolognese sauce with a wooden spatula. Her feet were killing her after a day cutting hair at one of the old people's homes in the town. It was relatively lucrative but took all of her stamina and patience to last 8 hours with petulant and often rude and abusive elderly people. She was tired and was unable to rally to her husband's ebullient mood. Not only that but she was totally bemused by his enthusiasm.

"You could work in a top salon. Set up your own business. I don't know but hair is hair, isn't it? It needs cutting wherever you are in the country. In fact, you wouldn't even have to work full time if you didn't want to. Pick your clients, be exclusive."

Steve had no idea whether any of this was possible but he wasn't going to be deterred from his dream. He wanted this promotion; he had worked for it and he wanted his family on board and coming along for the ride with him. His wife's voice broke into his aspirational thoughts. At first, he wasn't quite sure that he had heard correctly but when he looked up, he knew he had.

"No" Lorraine with her arms crossed belligerently, turned away from the stove, and looked balefully at him "I'm not moving".

The elation started to drain from Steve's body. He rallied and tried again with the tactic that usually worked. In a wheedling voice he said: -

"Think of the kids. There would be so much for them to do. We could go out in the evenings more often as they get older. We could go to museums, the cinema – we could all get better educated…." His voice trailed off as he looked pleadingly into his wife's eyes.

She looked scornful. "Museums? Since when you have ever been interested in visiting museums?"

"Lorraine, please don't be like that. This is a really good opportunity for me, and the money will benefit all of us. I've worked hard for this promotion and I don't want to turn it down. If I do, I know there will never be another chance." He couldn't help the note of desperation that crept into his voice.

Lorraine's gaze flicked briefly to a magazine cover lying open on the work surface. It showed the immaculate sun lit house of a famous Hollywood actress. She wanted to live there, not here and not in an unknown city. Guiltily she moved her eyes back to her husband's face, but it was too late.

One month later Steve started getting up at 5.30 in the morning to catch an early train for the first of his many two-hour commutes.

Some days when he opened the train door either in the city first thing in the morning or back home later in the evening, he felt that he was stepping into an entirely different world. Ostensibly, he fitted in when he stepped onto the platform in the morning. He wore a smart suit, carried a briefcase, sometimes an overcoat over his arm, had shiny black lace up brogues and a subtle stylish tie done up to the neck. Men and women dressed similarly and smartly swarmed in and out of the train station. Everyone in a hurry to get to their respective important job or open plan office. Steve wouldn't admit it but he loved being part of the great British workforce. The energy and sense of purpose was infectious. He felt part of something bigger and self-importance filled him with confidence.

The work wasn't as hard as he had feared, and he coped well but the commute took its toll on relationships within the office. The networking as they were now obliged to call it! He would have loved to join the 5-a-side football team or go for a drink after work to celebrate somebody's birthday but if he did, and he had at first, he didn't get home until 10 or 11 o'clock at night to find his wife and children fast asleep in bed. He was then up before them and back on the train which he wished he had slept on. Those were the times when he felt he was on a treadmill but the roar of the city as he stepped off the train always put him in a better mood.

In the evenings the crumpled, weary, bank manager opened the front door to what he came to call slovenliness in his head. His heady arrogance replaced by a sinking feeling. The house was always untidy, littered with shoes and clothes discarded where they had been removed. Magazines and papers stacked in the corner of the hall along with flyers for the local pizza emporium and the obligatory double-glazing pamphlets. Cups and mugs lined the stairs and wet towels hung over the bannisters. The sight of the kitchen always made his heart sink into his boots. Unwashed plates stacked precariously on the draining board and the sink filled with scummy brown water, cutlery and bowls. The difference between his two lives was stark. He left behind shiny chrome, gleaming windows, high-heeled tight-skirted secretaries, talk of the FTSE and Dow Jones in walnut panelled boardrooms for, and he wasn't going to beat about the bush here, pure squalor.

His wife and children took no interest in his appearance through the front door or his work. They carried on bickering, shouting or if he was lucky, watching TV as if he didn't exist. He was gone for so many hours of the day that to them he was almost a figment of their imaginations. The invisible man who kept the bank balance topped up, the lawn mown in the summer and cut the Turkey at Christmas, the one day of the year they all managed to be civil to each other. Boxing day was another story.

At the party Steve stood watching the two women on the dance floor jigging and shaking. The same fringed bobbed hairstyle – not that he recognised it as such. One golden, now bottle, blonde the other a glossy chestnut brown. They moved and weaved, arms flailing and hips swaying in time to the beat. He recognised the tune as something by George Michael but he couldn't be sure of its title. Each woman appeared oblivious to the other.

Al appeared at his side and shouted in his ear "She looks good, doesn't she?". Steve turned his head sharply.

"Who?"

"Laura – I spoke to her outside. Doing well for herself. Good job, nice house, nice car"

Steve looked blankly at his friend then shrugged his shoulders. He hadn't heard a word above the throbbing music. Al shouted even louder directly into Steve's ear.

"The dark-haired woman dancing next to Lorraine – that's Laura Coombs – well, she's married now – but that's her".

Steve swung around to gaze towards the dance floor just as the music changed to a slower tune. He barely had time to notice Laura when his vision was filled with his wife tottering towards him in her too tight low cut dress and overly high heels. A light bulb went off in his head and he felt physically sick because he knew what she had become.

Chapter 13 – Forty-five   2006

Tom was sat on the edge of Laura's desk, one foot on the floor and the other dangling in mid-air as if he was riding a horse side-saddled. The top button of his white shirt was undone, and his tie knot sat just below it. His sleeves were rolled up and he looked as if he had had a hard day's work. He was pinging elastic bands into the metal wastepaper bin at slow but regular intervals.

"So" he was saying "I'll probably have a pizza then I'm going to sit in front of the TV with a bottle of beer and watch the football in my underpants. What do you think?" He asked Laura purposely saying things to shock "Do you want to join me? We could have some fun at half time if you like?" he grinned lasciviously.

"Hmmm, tempting" Laura murmured. She had her eyes glued to her screen and was typing at an extremely fast pace.

Tom suggested an exotic or erotic, depending on your point of view, evening's entertainment to her just about every night that he was in the office. When she first knew him, she was a bit taken aback by his brazen audacity and gave indignant replies about being married and having children. She soon realised that he was all talk. He couldn't resist glancing at, commenting on or chatting up any attractive woman that walked past him. He did like Laura he made no bones about that but he never stopped going on about it which was a well-known way of showing he would never do anything about it. She could not deny that it was very flattering to have a younger man in her thrall even if most of it was a show. In fact, they were very good friends. Good enough for Laura to have confided that her marriage left a lot to be desired and for Tom to realise that she flourished with a little flattery. Not that it was a hardship for him. At 45 she passed for 10 years younger. Her figure was good, her hair stylish and modern as was her dress sense. After a while, when Laura knew Tom's ostentatious propositions were going to be a regular occurrence, she had looked up synonyms of enticing so that she could have a witty and urbane answer to hand. There turned out to be only one so she alternated between tempting and enticing. Tonight, it was the turn of 'tempting', she was pretty certain she had used 'enticing' the night before!

Tom was Laura's junior by 8 years, but they were equals at work. Each of them managing a team of 9 people. When the positions had been created a few years earlier, Tom had expected to get one and Laura had not. Thrown together for courses and meetings they became friends. Tom thought, for an older woman, Laura was very attractive and Laura thought the same about Tom but treated him with mild disdain which encouraged rather than deterred him to be outrageous. He had a gorgeous long-haul air stewardess girlfriend whom he adored but saw very infrequently. Laura privately thought that if she wasn't a figment of his imagination, she could probably be around a lot more than she was but any vaguely derogatory comment brought out Tom's defensive streak, so she gave the subject a wide birth. Not that this stopped Tom from commenting on every aspect of Laura's life that he felt warranted attention. Nevertheless, she enjoyed Tom's attentiveness and friendship; he sought her out and gave her ego a much-needed boost. They were good for each other.

Another elastic band pinged into the bin.

"Will you stop doing that?" Laura snapped, hands in mid-type. "I'm trying to concentrate"

"Okay Mrs Miles, keep your hair on" Tom took no notice of her moodiness. "Come on talk to me – what are you doing this weekend?"

"I'm trying to finish this email – it's important and I want to have a job to come to on Monday morning so just shut up for a minute!"

Laura typed on for 5 minutes, sat back scanned the screen again, added a couple of commas and pressed send. Quickly she turned all her devices off, stood up and turned to face Tom.

"The same as ever, I expect"

"Ice man not taking you out for a romantic meal then?" Tom smirked. Laura sighed.

"Tom, you ask me that every weekend and every Friday I give you the same answer. I live vicariously through my children. Thank goodness they have friends that have parents that invite me in for wine or coffee when I pick them up from sleep overs and parties otherwise, I would be a lonely old spinster with no social life."

"Hardly a spinster! You can't be a spinster – you're married!"

Laura dipped her head and looked up at Tom through her eyelashes. "There are three people in this marriage, so it's a bit crowded" she paraphrased Princess Diana "and the other woman is called Yamaha".

Tom started to laugh "It's such a waste" he said. "You are still gorgeous despite your age"

"Thank you so much" Laura was mock gracious "I will remind you of that when you are an old and decrepit 45-year-old but I don't have two wheels or handlebars so am not interesting enough."

"Don't fish! One compliment will have to do for now. You know you are interesting. We have all sorts of interesting conversations"

"Hmm" Laura stood up and put on her jacket "mostly about whether or not I want to watch you eat something disgusting semi-naked"

"You wouldn't have to be semi-naked" Tom deadpanned "I was going to be semi-naked, but I wouldn't say no if you took your clothes off, too".

Laura laughed, shrugged her jacket on over her cream shirt and picked up her hand bag. "I'm off. I'll text you. Enjoy the football". Her heels clicked on the tiled floor as she walked towards the lift leaving Tom to admire her rear view.

Chapter 14 – Forty-five

As Laura had walked off the dance floor ten years earlier Steve Miles was still staring in the direction from where she had come. He hadn't been watching her at all. When she got to the bar and the relative safety of her husband's company she looked back. He was dancing with the woman in the tight white dress. She realised that it must have been Lorraine Carter that was. Lorraine Miles now, of course. She hadn't recognised her. Not that Laura had known her very well at school but the weight she had gained had somehow changed the shape of her face. Steve's body language was not that of a man enjoying what he was doing. He held her at arm's length shuffling around in a perfunctory circle rather ironically to 'Once, twice, three times a lady' with a face like thunder.

When they got home, Laura thought she and Steven might have sex as they often did. Sometimes the shared intimacy made her feel that there was some value in their marriage, that they didn't lead parallel lives under the same roof. At other times it had the reverse effect leaving her feeling little better than a prostitute the speed and efficiency with which he reached his climax turned over and went to sleep. That night he had stayed downstairs to watch a late-night bike race with a cup of coffee, and she had gone to bed alone. She didn't mind, did she? Of course, not said the dutiful wife.

A few years later when Tom had started dissecting Laura's marriage and she had told him about the night. He had said "Well, you only have yourself to blame".

"Why?" she had exclaimed.

"You should have lured him up the stairs"

"How? I didn't have any 'Eau de Castrol' at the time!"

"Oh, come on, I am sure you could have thought of something. Or didn't you really want to?" Tom arched an eyebrow.

"It wasn't that. He should have known. Why couldn't he just think for himself? Think about how I might be feeling and not just about what he wanted?"

"Oh, you ladies!" said Tom chidingly "You read too much romantic fiction and credit us with more emotional sense than we've got. Those stories are more wishful thinking written by women than reality. We need leading by the nose and don't have the psychological maturity or sensitivity required to work out what is going on in your heads".

"That is such hard work" Laura sighed "I just can't be bothered".

"Welcome to our world!" Tom quipped.

Chapter 15 – Forty-five

The prize took Laura by surprise. She had been on the short list for 'Colleague of the year' ("Why can't we just get on with our jobs and go home?" She bemoaned. "Because then management wouldn't get to feel pious and patronizing" Tom replied) but never expected to win it. Sat by Tom in the 300 strong audience of the converted board room she was completely taken aback when her name was called out and it took her a couple of minutes to stumble out of the row of seats and walk down the aisle towards the podium to receive the prize. There were six finalists, all men except for her, some of whom had done some impressive things during the year like organising the obligatory 'fun' days for charity or coming up with the new advertising idea. As far as she was concerned all she had done all year was a steady job and help to win three very big lucrative accounts – one being with their new advertising agency.

"Your right" said Tom laughing "You did nothing, you don't deserve it. It was a token woman thing. Give it to me!"

Despite the grandeur of the occasion the prize in Tom's view was not as good as it was extolled considering they worked for a multi-million-pound company. Laura was not so ungrateful and sagely put nearly all the £2000 prize money into her pension fund and accepted the meal voucher with good grace.

Steven was genuinely really pleased and even the now 15-year-old twins managed to extricate themselves from their respective bedrooms and computer games to congratulate her. Her husband on the other hand was nowhere near so keen to join her for the expensive dinner in a top-notch restaurant. Tom had no so such qualms and readily volunteered his services. She pleaded and tried bargaining with Steven all to no avail.

"You know I hate all that dressing up and fancy food and waiters putting napkins on your lap."

"You should be so lucky" Laura tried to lighten the mood. "Okay, I get it, but it would only be for a few hours and I want to go with you. Please come." She wheedled knowing it was futile.

"Can't your gay friend go with you?"

"Who?" Laura knew who he meant "Tom? Well, yes, I suppose so but that isn't really the point. It is supposed to be a treat for us not an employee's night out and you know full well that he's not gay".

"He's not? Are you sure?"

Laura had told Steven on many occasions that Tom wasn't gay but he chose to ignore the fact. It allowed him to justify another man taking his still attractive wife out for dinner when, and he knew this, it should have been him. He wasn't jealous, not really, because he didn't belong in Laura's work world and didn't want to but he wished she didn't have quite such a willing replacement, either.

He explained again that he did not feel comfortable in places like that and did not want to go. Besides he said, somebody needed to stay with the children. Laura was determined this would not turn in to another row or what passed for one. She was really tired of them. Him stating his case and mutely refusing to change his mind, her screaming and shouting and getting nowhere. The baby-sitting excuse had been a first and it turned out a last! It was normally Laura who made all the arrangements around child care if she was not providing it herself. Steven being either too tied up with his business ("I'm self-employed, love, always something to do") or visiting with Laura's love rival Mrs Yamaha. Laura knew that if he was going to resort to child-care as an excuse, he was never going to be persuaded to go so gave up.

The restaurant was right up Tom's alley. It was within a smart up-market hotel which was situated on the side of a hill overlooking the town. The exterior had up-lighters focusing on the front of the Georgian mansion which made it look even more grand than it was and it was pretty grand. The dining room was lit by star-like sparkling lights in the ceiling and small old-fashioned table lamps. The crisp white tablecloths and napkins blended stylishly with the golden coloured chair covers and small indoor trees decorated with fairy lights gave the impression of eating outside on a warm spring day. One side of the room was a glass wall which overlooked the valley with its twinkling lights and necklace of traffic wending its way to destinations unknown. Laura stood in the doorway for a few minutes and took it all in. She knew one thing for sure Steven would have hated it.

A waiter led Tom and Laura to their table near the window and took their drinks order. Gin and tonic for Laura and a lemonade for Tom. He had agreed to drive as it was Laura's prize night. Steven had chatted companionably with Tom from underneath the latest motorbike that he was restoring when he had popped his head around the garage door. They didn't have much in common but there was no animosity either. Steven sent Tom on his way with a warning to ensure that Laura had a good time and wiped his greasy hand on a rag before pecking Laura on the lips. Tom turned his head away and bit his tongue rather than give the reply he would have liked to have.

"Did you finish that report on time" enquired Tom as he opened the menu.

"No work talk," said Laura "but, yes, I did".

Laura fished for her glasses that she had just rather annoyingly started wearing and began to mentally work out the calories of each dish. The chicken sounded nice but a cream sauce on a school night that was not good. She would have to pound the treadmill for more minutes than she had time for, in the morning, if she ate that. No, it would have to be something else. Fish, that was low in calories but she didn't like it much and didn't want to force it down her throat on a special night. She continued looking up and down, mentally calculating until she settled on a vegetarian option with goat's cheese, spinach and some other legume-type ingredients. If she ate that and no bread there was a possibility of a low- calorie pudding assuming the restaurant did such a thing. It was rather annoying that they weren't all on the same menu because at the local pub she worked backwards from the treacle sponge and custard to the single lettuce leaf and half a tomato salad. This place was too posh for that – people who came here did not need to watch their weight. They all had enough money to get any fat they put on sucked straight back off them again.

"I can't believe Steven did not want to come here! Did you never do anything like this when you were going out or celebrating something exciting like fixing a gearbox?" Tom's animated voice interrupted Laura's mental arithmetic.

"No, never" Laura debated being disloyal and decided that she would be "Steven's idea of a posh restaurant is a bikers café that has one item on the menu that isn't deep fried".

Tom grinned. "Is the Iceman really that unsophisticated? Why on earth did you marry him?"

Laura asked herself that at least twice every day and always came to the same conclusion. It seemed like a good idea at the time. It wasn't that they had an unhappy marriage just one where they had little in common and revolved around each other in different orbits. They didn't hate each other but they weren't love's young (or not so young any more) dream either. There just seemed to be a vacuum in their marriage where companionship, and a deep feeling of belonging to each other should be. But did she want romance and sex every night and going to the shops hand in hand? No, she didn't want that either. All that effort! She wasn't sure what it was that she did want.

"No marriage talk" Laura was firm.

Tom looked, quizzically, at her over the menu. "Then what the hell are we going to talk about? Are you going to ban gossip, too?"

"Don't be daft" said Laura laughing "I'm not completely insane. We could talk about your relationship. Which country is the lovely Nicole in tonight?"

"Singapore, I think. Can't be sure, I lose track of the time zones then her movements. She is on her way to or from Australia, I know that much. There is not much else to say. She is very lucky to have me" he deadpanned.

"She actually is. A lot of men would not put up with their women being away so much" Laura remarked.

"I'm one of those new-fangled men who can push a hoover and use the washing machine I don't need a woman for those things"

"I had heard that the lesser-spotted domesticated man did exist but I have yet to find one. Who ….." Laura tailed off. Tom was staring across the room.

"Isn't that Katrine over there?"

"Katrine?" Laura looked puzzled.

"Katrine Bosko. The Polish girl in Simon's team. Long blonde hair, very pretty, big…".

"Careful!"

"Eyes, Laura, eyes! Get your mind out of the gutter!"

Laura laughed but didn't get to look as at that moment a waiter arrived and with immaculate impersonal manners took their orders, retrieved the menus and checked if they needed anything before heading for the kitchen.

"She's with an older man by the look of it. I wonder what they're doing here?" Tom continued after ordering pate and a medium rare steak to follow and Laura had skipped the starter and settled for a Waldorf salad.

"It's probably her rich ruggedly handsome father" said Laura without looking "and I'm a lot older than you and it is none of our business!"

"I know, I'm being nosy" Laura wondered fleetingly at that point whether he was gay. His penchant for gossip and drama completely outstripped hers. "they're holding hands across the table" Tom was straining to see what was going on "which isn't really something you do with your dad is it?"

"No, it's not" sighed Laura, thinking that her friend was showing an inordinate amount of interest in a beautiful girl from another department considering he was so happy with Nicole, and glanced around to where Tom was looking. She recognised the young lady as the aforementioned Katrine from the office, she was hard to miss, but she also recognised the curls on the collar of the older man, who had his back to her. It was not Katrine's father.

Chapter 16 – Forty-Five

On the walk back from the train some nights Steve had fantasised about leaving Lorraine. After that dreadful party when his wife had looked so classless and inelegant, he wondered what he had ever seen in her. He didn't recognise the pretty young girl that used to sit on the wall and distract him from football in any way at all. He knew he had changed, too, but in his eyes, it was for the better. He never expected to climb the corporate ladder as far as he had but he enjoyed it and the standing that it gave him in society. None of his friends had done badly in life, which he was genuinely pleased about, but none had done as well in their careers as he had. All of that made him feel a little self-important and smug until the train started to slow down for his station and his stomach churned at the thought of going home. To the outside world he kept up the pretence of a happy family life but his relevance beyond the white front door became less and less obvious. He was the bank manager at work and at home and nothing else!

Lorraine did not interest him in any way. They had nothing in common, rarely slept in the same bed and spent most evenings apart once they had exchanged the perfunctory news of the day. The children had gone off to university, for which Steve was grateful because at least they stood a chance of a decent career, but although he had hated the persistent noise and shouting, the silence was even worse. His fortieth birthday came and went but it took two more years before he had the courage to go.

One Friday evening as Steve got to his gate the thought of congealed food was too much for him and instead of turning in, he walked right on past. He longed, yes, really longed, to open his front door to a neat, clean and tidy house. His wife, casually but carefully dressed, calling "Hi, darling, how was your day?" and the sound of the fridge door opening and the top coming off a bottle of beer. As he entered the mood lit kitchen, music would be playing quietly and the smell of a pasta dish would give him hunger pangs. The table would be laid ready for a cosy supper with a crisp salad and newly baked bread in a basket beside the cruet. He would kiss his wife, pleased that this was the reward for a long hard week at work. Over the meal they would talk, intimately or about some work difficulties that he was facing or a problem she wanted him to help her solve then watch an hour of television before going to bed ready to wake up to a whole weekend of family time, catching up with friends and as much sport as he could find time to watch. Knowing full well his fantasy was exactly that, he kept walking until he passed a take-away where he picked up a big bag of Cod and chips and carried on until he got to his father's house. His dad was not surprised to see him. "I was wondering how much more you would put up with" he said matter-of-factly, as they sat in companionable silence chewing on the food.

By Saturday lunchtime Steve had 36 text messages from Lorraine and he hadn't replied to any of them. He talked everything through with his dad who agreed he could stay with him until he found somewhere else then finally sent one message to his wife. It said, 'We're done'.

The divorce was predictably messy but, Steve reflected ironically to Al, that Lorraine seemed to like messy so it must have suited her down to the ground!

Steve rented a flat on the other side of town, made an effort to have a relationship with his children, visited his father at least twice a week and after a year or so met Katrine Bosko on the train. He hadn't been on the look-out for somebody new and he reflected afterwards that was probably why they had found each other. Life was contrary like that. He hadn't been looking because he really enjoyed living on his own. The flat was always clean and tidy, he ate more fruit and vegetables, did more exercise, and went to the pub more often just to counteract the overall healthiness of his life. He even hooked up with Mandy on a couple of occasions but back at her place while her lorry driver husband was away and not at the back of the pub as they had before. That relationship was never going anywhere and they both knew it.

Katrine had quite literally fallen at Steve's feet! They had both been stood in the aisle of the overcrowded train as it came into the home station when it jolted like they do, and she had lost her balance. Her ankle buckled over on one of her vertiginous heels and she staggered sideways. Steve hadn't been able to see the face of the young woman stood in front of him but had been taken with the stylish hair-cut and the fresh smell of her perfume, when he was called upon to help. From behind, he grabbed the girl's elbow to steady her. After regaining her balance, she turned to thank her rescuer and Steve got a good look at his future girlfriend. He instantly knew that she was way out of his league but also that he wasn't going to let that stand in his way. She had clearly been crying recently but was nevertheless stunning with large blue eyes, long blonde hair and a voluptuous figure. Her clothes of dark grey skirt suit and pink blouse were office wear and along with the designer brief case meant, he deduced, that she must be on her way home from work.

"Are you hurt?" he asked solicitously.

"No, I am okay" Katrine replied rounding the O vowel the way the Polish do. "Damn..." she looked at Steve for approval and he nodded "trains. Yes, damn trains". She rolled her R's and smiled. Seductively, Steve decided. Definitely seductively.

The train lurched to its final halt and Katrine hung on with two hands to the head rest of a seat which contained an old man in a beige mac who seemed highly delighted to have such an attractive woman rubbing up so close to him.

Steve followed the young woman off the train and up the stairs, where he hastily made a decision. Walking quickly to draw alongside her he said,

"Can I buy you a drink? To calm your nerves." he finished lamely.

She looked taken aback but decided that her nerves, although there wasn't much wrong with them, could always benefit from a glass of wine and accepted. Steve was also taken aback, not expecting the conquest to have been quite so easy.

After a short walk to the pub and a long wait at the bar they settled themselves on stools in a dark corner and Katrine told Steve how she had just found out by text that the long-term boyfriend she had left behind in Poland was seeing somebody else. "Not just somebody else" she spat "Paulina, my best friend, Paulina" and tears started to fall again. Steve provided a comforting, metaphorical shoulder to cry on, friendly sympathy and arms-length respect. After an hour when Katrine had not called him grandad or alluded to his age once and he had found out her life story, happy but poor childhood just outside Olsztyn, university, moved to England for work, Katrine typed her number into Steve's phone. She thought he was cool handing her the latest Nokia but he had already decided that it was the safest way not to show his technological ignorance and they went their separate ways.

Two months later they were seeing each other three nights a week and Steve's mates were extremely jealous. Trust him to come out of divorce smelling of roses! Lucky bastard!!

Chapter 17 – Forty-five

Tom missed nothing including the look on Laura's face as she saw the man sat at the table on the other side of the room.

"Do you know him?" He asked then seeing a look on Laura's face that he didn't recognise answered his own question "you do know him. I can tell".

Laura took a sip from her glass in an effort to disguise the rush of emotion she was feeling and to calm her churning stomach. What was he doing here? Why did he rear his head periodically throughout her life? And why did the man still disturb her so much? Yet again, he made her feel inept, inadequate and small and 15 years old. He, on the other hand, looked successful, smart and clearly attractive to the much younger opposite sex. Objectively Laura could see why. He had aged well and could have passed for one of those ruggedly handsome self-deprecating film stars. As she gazed at him Steve turned his head and raised his arm to summon the waiter. His white shirt sleeve was turned back twice revealing a strong wrist and an expensive looking metal-strapped watch. Seeing his profile took her thoughts back to the Maths classroom, what seemed like ages before, and with a jolt like snorting cocaine (she imagined) or injecting adrenalin directly into a vein she felt a desire that she hadn't felt for years. A sexual flame that had been long buried ignited with such ferocity that despite everything she had to confront the fact that she still wanted him. Nobody she had met since had ever had the same effect on her. Not since she was 15 years old! As she watched from a distance, she knew with absolute certainty that she wanted it to be her hand he was holding, her eyes he was looking in to and she hated herself for it. Had she learnt nothing about herself? About him? What was the matter with her? Where was her self-esteem? She didn't believe all this nonsense about loving people who treated you badly! Why would you yearn for somebody who treated you like that? Why indeed?

She hated him and she hated herself and she hated the girl that was in his thrall. And yet she wanted him more than ever before.

Laura had heard the small-town gossip from Jane about Steve's unpleasant divorce and Lorraine's vitriol but hadn't realised that life had turned out so well for him.

Eventually, in a strangled voice she managed to reply to Tom "We, um, we went to the same school" and this time took a big slug from her glass.

"You did? I was beginning to think he was a mass murderer you had just recognised" Tom raised an eyebrow then realised that a joke was not going to go down well at that moment so kept quiet. After a while she said,

"He ...um... we had a couple of classes together."

Tom could tell that there was more to it but also knew better than to ask so decided on the humorous route after all and said "He looks much younger!"

Laura smiled thinly. "He always did".

"That was a joke, Laura" Tom wasn't sure where all this was going. "You know you look great. I wouldn't be seen out with you if you didn't". He smiled to indicate that it was another joke.

Laura didn't return it. Tom was finding her hard work.

"Do you want to talk about him or whatever the problem is he causes? I'm a captive audience tonight and you might not get another chance".

Laura wasn't sure whether she could. The pain and the humiliation were part of her DNA now and not something to be cut out and recounted as an anecdote or analysed by somebody else. It had shaped her – she acknowledged that although it did not make her grateful. If she did talk, shouldn't she be telling her husband? After all he was the one, she should share everything with not a man who really was nothing but a work colleague however well they got on. She wouldn't know where to start. Would it be with the ridicule Steve had subjected her to or earlier than that when she thought of him as a friend and he didn't think of her at all or at the point where she had made a complete fool of herself? She didn't know. No, however much she and Tom got on it was because of their professional relationship at work and she didn't want that ruined. If he saw her as somebody not to look up to then the foundation of their friendship would fall apart. Their jokey quasi – intimate relationship was based on mutual respect and that is how she wanted it to remain. She was not going to make herself look weak or vulnerable in front of him, her husband or anybody else. She was never going to talk about it, to anyone. The pain, even after all the years hurt like nothing she had ever experienced and she shut the door on it. She'd lived, she'd learned and she had survived. Laura switched back on.

"There is nothing important to say" she smiled warmly at Tom "It's years since I was at school and I barely remember anything about it". She turned away and gazed out of the window and he knew better than to ask anything more.

Steve was too old to hold hands at the table even with a woman as beautiful as Katrine. He was dining with her – there was nothing else he needed to prove. Katrine had other ideas so hold hands they did. They had been seeing each other for two years and at 32, Katrine, who despite her tears when they met had very rapidly started calling her ex 'that bastard Lukasz' rolling her tongue spitefully over the R in bastard, wanted to get married and have children. Steve had no intention of going down that road again. In an effort to placate her he had booked the expensive restaurant for her birthday but knew that it would be a difficult evening because despite her constant hints and, sometimes, blatant threats, he was not going to give in. He hoped the ambience of the place and frankly mind-blowingly over-priced menu would put her in a good mood and she would not create a scene when the present in a small box was not the one, she was hoping for. He knew he was kidding himself.

There were two sides to having a much younger, stunning-looking girlfriend. His friends envied him; he gained more friends. Male work colleagues looked on him with respect and female ones flirted openly as he suddenly changed from being dull old Steve to fanciable Steve. His looks changed from being aging to rugged, his clothing from boring to sartorial, and his conversation from mundane to witty. Steve liked the person he had become to the outside world. Behind closed doors it all wore him out! Katrine was high maintenance; she wanted to go out several times a week to interesting places and expected him to locate these places then be her suave and attentive escort. She spent hours getting ready and expected sex before and after the outings. She was fun and interesting and full of energy when all Steve wanted was a pint at the pub with his mates and nights in front of the television watching football. But more than anything what he wanted was not to get married and have children for a second time.

Chapter 18 – Fifty-five - 2016

The autumn sun hung low in the sky shining through the dying leaves creating a riot of colour above Laura's head as she walked. Beneath her feet was a golden and burnished carpet where the leaves had fallen onto the pavement and were slowly changing to mush. She had walked this same route at least once a week, often more, for over a year. The first few times were in conditions similar to this, later the trees had been bare, the weather cold and crows had cawed mournfully from high in the sky where they floated on the thermals. The spring walk with daffodils lining the paths and blossom on the trees was her favourite time but summer followed that and August loomed closer.

There was a smell of newly mown grass as she entered the cemetery. Somebody had driven a ride-on mower between the graves in an attempt to keep the plot looking tidy. Many of the newer graves had vases of fresh flowers on them, cheery amongst grey mildewy headstones. A few had teddy-bears or football scarves others had dead flowers sat in a jam-jar containing brown water with the stalks toppling over at untidy angles. Laura walked further along the gravel path until she got to the newer graves. Despite the lovely weather there was only one other person in the graveyard. They were stood in the shadows of the trees at the far end and Laura took very little notice. She passed a newly dug plot with a huge mound of earth beside it and assumed there was going to be a funeral the next day. Stopping at her destination she stared at the simple granite stone with the words she never expected to read and experienced the feeling of disbelief that had got milder as the year progressed.

In loving memory of

Steven Albert Knowles

Beloved husband, father and son

Died 30 August 2015 aged 54

Laura had felt very tempted to put AKA St Gregarious alongside his name but knew she was being facile. She was the only one that realised he had an alter ego – everybody else thought St Gregarious was the real Steven. That was the hardest part about being a widow – finding the appropriate words and emotions when required. Everybody expected her to be devastated and initially when the police officers insisted that she sat down in their snug little sitting room whilst they broke the news, she supposed she was but quite soon afterwards she wasn't but she still had to act as if she was. It wasn't that she didn't care about her husband or love him but they had lived parallel lives, neither of them needing much in the way of support – emotional, monetary or physical from the other. They were each self-reliant and after so many years she was used to it. Of course, the twins had been devastated but after the initial shock even they got back on with their lives. Steven had spent so much time in the garage with his beloved bikes that they had got used to him not being in the house. In one of life's ironies, it was the thing that he loved the most that brought about his demise. A car pulled out of a side turning veered onto the wrong side of the road and hit Steven's bike head on. He died instantly.

Steven's mother, Grace, was surprisingly unsurprised. "I blame Barry Sheene" she said. "Isn't he dead?" Laura replied. "He is now" said Grace "but from the time his dad took Steven to see him race, that was it – bikes were his life and now.." the impact of her loss began to take hold and her voice was wracked with sobs "they have caused his death".

Grace had not been in good health and the weight of her grief brought on an earlier end than might have been expected. Her grave was two rows behind that of her son's.

There was a bench at the far end of the graveyard with a metal plaque in remembrance of a couple that had died two years beforehand. Laura walked to it and sat down. Her mind drifted to thoughts of the last few years of her marriage. As the children had grown up, she and Steven had the opportunity to go out. On the bike, or a bike – there had been many, but they had some fun times visiting picturesque towns or cathedrals. Around bikes was where he had felt most comfortable and if she felt they were close it was those times when she was perched as a pillion behind him peering over his shoulder, watching the road and waiting to copy his exact movements. The loss of her mother five years previously had shown that they weren't.

At the time of the devastating stroke her mother had suffered Laura had taken care of the practical things. Her father had been away and after the third unanswered phone call in 15 minutes she became worried. She had found her mother slumped on the kitchen floor; a mug of tea spilt over the tiles. The paramedics had arrived quickly but Laura knew from their body language that things were not going to end well and two days later, her mother died. Steven initially had been solicitous and helped Laura and her father with the funeral arrangements but as her grief took hold and her mood depressed, he resumed his residency in the garage. On bad days she trotted down the garden, parked herself on a tool box and talked to the pair of feet she could see poking out from under a bike. The feet grunted occasionally but offered nothing that Laura could take solace from so she stopped going. St Gregarious had no compassionate alter ego it appeared or if so, he was not available to Laura. Her father's life did not alter course very much and she heard little from him – she knew he had a parallel world but didn't pursue it.

In another one of life's twists Tom had married Katrine and produced a baby. The lovely air stewardess had stopped coming home and he had finally admitted to himself that the romance was dead. After realising that he had wasted a number of years waiting in vain he pursued the opposite sex with a vengeance. Laura was treated to an endless diatribe on who he had found on Tinder and which way he had swiped. His one-track mind became grindingly dull although a tiny part of her wished she had some excitement in her life. He had got together with Katrine after he had met her on a train when she was returning from an audit. The train had jolted, she had lurched on her high heels and this time Tom had been her rescuer. A couple of months after a glass of wine and Katrine's life story in a nearby pub they had become an item. It appeared she had found a winning formula including referring to her ex as 'that bastard Steve'. Inevitably Tom drifted away from Laura both physically, as he rushed home to his family most nights instead of pinging elastic bands into her bin, and emotionally as his talk became more about nappies and night feeds and less football and innuendo. Laura missed it; she missed him. It took a while but Tom grew up.

Laura became even more self-reliant. There was nobody she could or wanted to turn to for emotional support so she didn't. Each night as she lay down on the pillow all the thoughts she didn't want to have and couldn't stop crowding into her brain were mentally put in a cupboard and locked away. It was the only way she could sleep - a deep dark dreamless sleep. On the day Steven died she hadn't realised he had gone out. At breakfast he had mentioned that the bike he was working on needed a good run so that he could check the gears or the engine or something. She didn't know, didn't understand and had barely listened; it was the same conversation all the time. With her headphones on she had hoovered the house and when she went to empty the dust into the bin realised, there was no bike in the garage.

After the policeman had delivered the tragic news and she had caught odd phrases like "so very sorry", "wrong side of the road" "died instantly" she couldn't remember what their last meaningful conversation had been about or when they had last had sex, or watched television together and guilt set in. She blamed herself for their empty marriage, for his death and everything in between. She convinced herself that she had single-handedly sabotaged their relationship with her stoicism, never allowing him to get too close in case he hurt her and yet he never had. Not really! He had just adjusted to her aloofness and it had played into his hands. She assuaged her guilt with her weekly walk to the graveyard, the added bonus being that she burnt off some calories. Steven wouldn't have minded, she decided, he had tolerated her daily rituals because he was in no position to argue with them. At times she almost laughed out loud at the reaMelanietion that his emotional presence had changed little. She was used to talking to her husband whilst he was under something and this time it was the ground.

Eyes closed, sunglasses on and lost in thought, Laura felt the bench judder and realised somebody else had sat down. She didn't want to be disturbed. The person said nothing so she stayed in her own world for a while longer until the sun dipped behind a tree and she felt its warmth disappear from her face. The air chilled and something in the atmosphere changed. She opened her eyes. The person on the bench was hidden inside a large black hoodie which hid their face but the build gave away that is was a man. She realised it was the person she had noticed in the distance when she first walked in to the cemetery. He wore black jeans and black leather gloves, like a terrorist, she thought and it scared her. There was no warmth around him. He didn't glance in her direction with a friendly nod but instead started a slow tap of his foot on the floor. Rhythmically, without moving any other muscles he kept going. Laura's skin prickled and she felt a cold hard stone land in the pit of her stomach. She recognised the feeling; it was fear. In that quiet, too quiet, graveyard she knew that she was in danger. She had an idea what the black clad stranger wanted and she didn't like it.

Laura took a deep breath as quietly as she could. She couldn't let this man see that she was afraid but she had to quickly work out a plan. Casually she looked around the grave yard hoping to give the impression that she was waiting for somebody but in reality, praying that somebody, anybody, would appear. The place remained resolutely empty as the shadows started to lengthen and the sun sank lower. The temperature dipped. The man's foot continued tapping relentlessly and slowly. Laura's heart was thudding in her chest as her alarm built. Realising that plan was not going to work and appearing to do the same thing as before she scanned around for the quickest way out. She had walked a long way down the path and was surrounded on three sides by hedges and overhanging trees which were throwing dark silhouettes onto the grass. Laura was trapped. The menacing beat continued. A relentless countdown to an unspeakable act. She had no choice but to run. She didn't think she would get far but she had to try.

Laura rose from the seat and began to walk back towards the gates. They seemed a long way off. Dusk was falling and it was difficult to pick them out but she knew they were there at the end of the evergreen and terrifyingly dark path. The man stayed put. Laura was surprised and had a split-second thought that perhaps she had built the whole unpleasant episode up in her head when the gravel behind her crunched and she knew he was walking too. She lengthened her stride determined not to run.

The noisy footsteps sped up and Laura realised the man was running. Running towards her and gaining fast. His breathing as loud in the still night air as if he was right behind her. With no pretence of bravado Laura screamed piercingly, pure fear getting the better of her, adrenalin coursing through her veins and she ran, too. Her trainers scooted about on the gravel as she gained and lost traction, breathing heavily and eyes straining to see the gates and what she considered to be relative safety. Outside in the street there had to be somebody around to help her – there just had to be otherwise, what? She couldn't think about it.

All of a sudden, as if she had reached the tape on school sports day the gates were in front of her and she flung herself through them, gasping for air as if she had won a race. She chanced a look over her shoulder as she dashed along the pavement towards a lighted window and crashed right into the arms of a man walking along with a bunch of flowers in his hand. Laura screamed, again. She was wracked with anxiety and her breath came in short gasps. She couldn't speak but silently thanked God for sending him to her.

The man spoke in an amused voice.

"And there was I thinking I was too old for women to thrown themselves at me!"

She didn't answer doubled over at the waist unable to catch her breath. That had not been a jog, it had been a full-scale sprint that Usain Bolt would have been proud of and she wasn't in the mood for jokes. She needed time to recover.

When Laura didn't reply the man changed his tone.

"What on earth has happened? Are you okay?" He leant over with his palm on her back in order to address the side of her face as she continued to pant. Laura wished he would stop asking stupid questions when she was in no state to respond. Her gratitude for being rescued waning quickly.

At the sound of another voice the footsteps behind her stopped and began to recede. Her gratitude returned. She was safe.

She gasped. "The light!"

"What? Light? What do you mean light?" The man's voice was bemused.

Laura headed for a lamp post where a pool of light spread out on the uneven, chewing gum, fag butt strewn pavement. She felt she had to get there to feel secure. It was the end of that frightening episode. She broke free of the man and walked hastily the 20 yards to it, leant heavily against the cold metal, closed her eyes and broke into sobs. She had made it, she felt safe.

The man had abandoned his bunch of flowers to the nearest grave just inside the gate which was over two hundred years old and the contents of which were less ashes to ashes and more dust of dust. Any living relatives, supposing there were any that visited, would have a shock to see that somebody had been thoughtful enough to remember their long dead relative. He turned followed her into the pool of light and stood, a little distance away, giving Laura time to compose herself. He hoped he was offering a comforting presence.

Laura felt her heartbeat slowing a little. The yammering in her chest and the pounding in her head not quite so loud. Unsteadily she stood up straight, the sobs of shock abating. Once, again, the concerned man asked.

"Are you okay? Do you need medical help? What on earth happened?"

Laura, calmer now, lifted her head to thank and reassure the man that she did not need a 6 hour wait in A&E. It was Steve Miles.

Chapter 19 – Fifty-five

The next morning, lying in bed after an unfamiliarly bad night's sleep, Laura reflected at the irony of running from the devil she didn't know into the arms of the devil she did.

Steve had been considerate and Laura in so much shock (at their meeting as much as the graveyard menace) that it didn't take much for him to guide her to the nearest pub, sit her down and purchase them each a drink. He was getting quite adept at this. He hadn't asked just walked back with a pint of something brown for him and a glass of wine for her. It was Shiraz which happened to be one of her favourites. He couldn't have known - it was just coincidence. Her hands were shaking and she spilt more than she drank but downed half-a-glass quickly then babbled about a man in a hood and his tapping foot. It all sounded a bit melodramatic and Hitchcockian to her but Steve took her seriously. He thought they should call the police but Laura had too many bad memories of those uniforms and couldn't face dealing with them again. Anyway, what could she tell them? A man that she couldn't identify of medium height, medium weight, ageless and faceless wearing a black hoodie had maybe tried to do something to her at the back of the graveyard. What something? She didn't know – it had just felt menacing. Perhaps he was on his usual evening walk and following women along tree-lined paths whilst in the throes of an asthma attack was something he considered a hobby? A weird one – it could, of course, be weirder but weird all the same. After half an hour or so the wine took hold and along with the warmth and safety of the pub and Steve's (she had to admit) reassuring presence her hands had stopped shaking.

Over the years of inventing possible scenarios where she would bump into Steve and, oh so casually, pretend, she hadn't realised it was him and with a little laugh dismiss his compliments about her looks or her achievements, running from a would-be attacker had not been one of them. Her favourite was when she envisaged a wedding of a mutual friend (not that she could think of any besides Jane and Kevin who had been married for around 200 years but that was a minor detail). Laura would be there on her own, by choice or design, didn't matter. She would be wearing a fitted floral, demure but edgily sexy dress, high heeled sandals and a little complementary fascinator atop her gloriously shiny dark hair. A group of people would be surrounding her in the garden of the country house where this fictitious wedding was taking place, laughing at her witty asides to the male protagonist's humorous story. At a particularly funny bit she would look away from the group across the immaculately groomed lawn and there he would be in a dark grey M&S suit, pink carnation in his button hole and curls, neat and tidy, resting on the collar of his white shirt. His blue eyes sparkling and amused, listening to the charming woman he had just spotted and realising that he knew her as that Laura girl from school that he had been so cruel to and had totally misunderstood. He would make amends. Without taking her eyes away from his gaze she would politely extricate herself from her group of urbane friends and walk across the grass towards him…….

The door-bell rang waking Laura from her reverie and putting a different and unwanted thought in her head. Who the hell was that at this ungodly of hour of, she checked the clock, 5 past 7"?

5 past 7? In the morning? Oh, good grief – she was late – very, very late for her exercise routine, and work. Oh no, not work – she had the day off, thank goodness for that. She hadn't set the alarm but normally she woke early anyway, her body clock set after years of running for trains and early rising young children. Thoughts of the previous evening returned and she assumed the shock had exhausted her but near-death experiences (who was getting carried away?) did not burn calories. She would get rid of this person as soon as possible and get on with it. It was probably a parcel – not that she could

remember ordering anything but perhaps one of the kids had forgotten to amend their address. She had calories to burn. A huge glass of white wine from the night before had to be got rid of. She needed to exercise!

Laura threw on a pair of running shorts, an old T-shirt, socks and trainers and pulled her hair into a short ponytail as she ran down the stairs. She could see a shadow she didn't recognise behind the glass so opened the door warily, on the defensive to shoo off whatever doorstep salesman or would-be local councillor awaited.

Steve stood on the doorstep holding two take-away cups of coffee in a cardboard holder. He was dressed for work and looked business-like in his suit and tie. Laura's first thought was that she hoped he had considered the environment when he had bought the coffee and the second was that she must look a wreck.

"Morning!" He was bright and cheerful "I was concerned about you after last night. You looked exhausted when I dropped you off and I just wanted to know that you had slept okay. Thought some coffee might help if you had slept too well". He laughed at his thin joke.

Laura's mind was racing. Another scenario that she hadn't envisaged. She felt obliged to invite him in, even though it put her whole morning out and she did not like being out of routine. She had a swift feeling of murderous anger towards her would-be attacker – look what he had triggered off. There was a severe danger that without her normal exercise she would wake up the next morning 10 stone heavier than she was now. In fact, this was actually her husband's fault because if he hadn't gone out on that stupid bike then he wouldn't be dead and she wouldn't have had to visit the graveyard in the first place. Olympic sized would-a, could-a, should-a thoughts raged through her head whilst Steve looked quizzically at her from the doorstep where he remained rooted to the spot.

"Um, yes, morning! Thank you. Very thoughtful" Laura was not a coffee person; it wouldn't get drunk. How could she appear grateful and get rid of him in one go? He looked as if he would like to come in so she said quickly, words tumbling out, "I'm in a rush now but would you like to go for a meal? Tomorrow evening? My treat. A way of thanking you properly – it's the least I can do." That bit wasn't true – it was just a polite thing to say – she could have done less; she could have done nothing.

Steve looked taken aback so she babbled on. "You don't have to, if you're busy or something?"

"No, no, I'm not. That would be really nice, thank you. It's a date"

Not a date thought Laura, a thank you. That was all, a thank you, she was nervous of the man. It had been years, she knew, and he had probably changed but she had seen him at his best and at his worst and her armadillo scales were armed and ready for action.

Chapter 20 – Fifty-five

After the night at the expensive restaurant, it had taken Katrine two more years to leave and even then, Steve had resorted to brutal and cruel tactics to make sure that she did. Eventually, he let rip with a vicious verbal attack designed to hurt. It worked. He hadn't meant to be so nasty but he had tried every other way to get across the fact that he wasn't going to marry her and he certainly wasn't going to have any more children with her or anybody. She continued to treat what he said as background noise, chatting endlessly on the phone to her friends about wedding dresses and children's names so that he knew he had to put a stop to it. After the row she got the message and stormed out of the house her high heels clattering noisily down the stairs but not drowning out a volley of Polish swear words that she spat at him over her shoulder. He wasn't bothered he had been called worse and if he hadn't, he didn't understand them anyway. They had a rancorous and bad-tempered split. She reacted badly and gave him a hard time by text until one day it all stopped. Through the grapevine he heard that she had fallen off her extraordinarily high heels on the train and had been rescued by a gallant and good-looking young man whom she ultimately married. Steve couldn't help but laugh. He was glad she had found what she was looking for. Although the end of their relationship had been hard it was nothing like as bad as his divorce and he still liked the girl. If he had met her in his twenties, he would have married her like a shot but he was adamant that he did not want to be a father again and ultimately that was what they argued about.

After Katrine's departure from his life, he became dull old Steve again. Women no longer wanted to flirt and the only people that invited him to the pub were his dad or Al. He didn't mind. This was what he needed, peace and quiet and the company of somebody who wanted the same thing as him.

Predictably Al told him he was a fool. He didn't think so. He enjoyed the nights with his father. They were close not in a tactile way but had an easy companionship that came from shared interests and a deep knowledge of each other. When his father died Steve realised that he had lost one of his two best friends.

Steve didn't often go to the cemetery on a Sunday or so late but on the way earlier in the afternoon he had got drawn into the pub when, through the window, he saw a football match on the big screen. He thought he would just have a quick half and watch a few minutes because he had nothing else to do. Several pints later and after having watched the home team win a 3-2 thriller, he thought he had better do what he had set out to do and go on down to the grave. He hadn't realised how dark it was outside and wouldn't have gone if he hadn't already bought the flowers. His mind was on the game and how much his father, Keith, would have enjoyed it.

Steve missed his father. He had been a non-judgemental support when he had moved back home after the end of his marriage. They enjoyed fishing or drinking or watching football side by side on the sofa with their feet on the coffee table and a can in their hands discussing the merits of England's midfield. Katrine had caused Keith to raise his eyebrows once or twice but he hadn't stopped his son moving out or moving back in again a few years later. He had laughed and said "Hard going the younger models, aren't they?" and his son had agreed. Keith had been in good health until the last year of his life when heart problems had slowed him down considerably and a heart attack ultimately killed him. Steve was glad for his father's sake that it had been quick but it had been a shock to find him stone cold in the chair when he got home from work. They had had their evening planned and it seemed such a shame.

As these thoughts were whirling around Steve's head, the last thing he expected was a human missile to hurtle through the graveyard gates and nearly knock him off his feet. Once he had understood through the gasping and panting that the, admittedly attractive, woman was terrified of something he was happy to play the heroic rescuer especially as he also heard the receding footsteps.

After he had walked Laura home and they had exchanged phone numbers using the excuse that Steve could check on her later in the evening, it came back to him who she was. He didn't really believe it.

This stylish, very attractive, slim, clearly intelligent woman could not possibly be the mousy, dull podgy girl from school. She just couldn't be. From the outside her house and garden had looked well kept and tidy, a year-old Range Rover parked in the drive. She obviously didn't lack funds. In the pub after Laura had calmed down, they had talked about normal things, the state of the local roads, music, weirdos in the graveyard, nothing too deep. Laura had been warm and witty and Steve liked her. It was nice to be with somebody who was his age group. Somebody to whom he didn't have to explain who Fleetwood Mac and Deep Purple were. He felt a connection between them. She gazed into his eyes just a fraction too long and when their hands had accidentally touched, he had felt a spark of desire.

Walking away from her house had made up his mind. Laura would be worth a shot. This, he decided could be his last chance of a relationship and if that was the case it was worth a little effort to win the big prize. He wanted to be envied by his friends, again and Laura could provide him with that. He would operate a charm offensive and it would start the following morning.

Chapter 21 – Fifty-five

Laura stared into her wardrobe hoping that something would jump out at her and the decision of what to wear for the meal with Steve would be taken out of her hands. The clothes were very unobliging so Laura continued to stare. The indecision was more down to the gamut of emotions that were coursing through her mind. Her 15-year-old self, had reappeared from the depths of her mind and started questioning the 55-year-old.

"What on earth are you doing?" 15-year-old Laura asked "Have you taken leave of your senses? Do you crave humiliation like a drug or something?"

"No" Fifty- five indignant – on the defensive.

"Well, what then?" 15 had got very defiant all of a sudden.

"The man saved me. I owe him a meal." Even to 55 this sounded lame.

"He didn't save you! You had got out of the graveyard. You would have been fine. Are you a masochist?"

Accidentally she supposed she was. The Accidental Masochist – that sounded like a good book title. if only she had an interesting story to go along with it.

"Well?" 15 was persistent.

"Leave me alone" 55 responded sulkily, feeling beleaguered.

"I won't leave you alone. You don't need a man to affirm that you are a good-looking intelligent woman"

"Oh, since when have you got so wise?" 55 was now on the offensive "Shame you didn't have that level of maturity when you actually were 15 then I might not be in the mess I am in now"

"Pah!" 15 was annoyed "Do what you want. Don't come running to me when he hurts you again. You are old enough to know better".

"I am old enough not to get hurt. It's not a date. It's just a companionable meal then I will never see him again".

"Oh, please!" 15 was scornful now "If you can't be honest with yourself who can you be honest with?".

The clothes in front of Laura belligerently refused to move and attach themselves to her body so she got up off the bed and chose a pair of jeans, a crisp white shirt, leather biker-style jacket, Chelsea boots and simple pearl stud earrings. If she was going then she would do it with as much style as she could muster.

In the doorway of the pub Laura's nerve nearly gave out. She would have turned and run if she had not caught sight of Steve in her favourite coloured, blue, shirt as he stood at the bar ordering a drink. She examined him from head to toe. He had aged, as they all had but he didn't look older than he should. His hair was much shorter now as was the fashion and was receding a little at the temples although the curls at the nape of his neck remained the same. He was thicker around the waist but not fat or paunchy as if he did a little to look after himself. His jaunty air remained and she felt the same attraction that she had all those years ago. She didn't want to, why couldn't her hormones have completely died when she had her menopause? Was it because she had spent so many years being starved of affection, coming in second to her father's other life, to Marcus who had just wanted her as his sex toy or to her husband whose first love had never been her? Would it matter if she had a fling with this man? Could her self-esteem which had been ground into the floor by his cruel words all those years ago really get any lower? After all she had achieved in reinventing her body and her mind why did she feel that she was a person that nobody could love?

At that moment he turned and saw her. He had chosen his shirt well because it reflected the blue of his eyes which did not look cold and steely but warm and welcoming.

As Laura walked through the door looking classy and stylish Steve knew he was doing the right thing. They would make a great couple. There was no irony in this thought he was only thinking of the here and now and the future, the past was gone and did not concern him.

Laura's stomach lurched as she saw him turn to greet her. Fear or anticipation she wasn't sure but it didn't have long to do a full floor routine with a triple somersault to finish, before Steve called out.

"Laura! Hi" he kissed her cheek "you look great. What can I get you? Wine, G&T?"

Drinks in hand they made for a table marked reserved in the corner of the pub. The room was dimly lit with candles on the table. Laura wondered idly whether she would be able to read the menu. Her eyesight wasn't what it had been and she needed a magnifying glass and flood-lights to read things these days. She needn't have worried the menus had unusually large print obviously catering for the older clientele that crowded the place at lunchtimes.

"How have you been?" asked Steve "any more graveyard encounters with nasty men?"

Laura laughed. "No, thank goodness. I am sure the kids think it was a figment of my imagination. When I face timed them, they did the raised eyebrow look which means Mum is off on one of her fantasies, again. Both of them, even though I called them separately!".

Steve couldn't picture Laura as a mother. She seemed too composed, despite the other night, to ever have changed nappies or mopped up sick. He couldn't imagine her house having been chaotic and messy like his family home had been.

"How old are your kids? "

"25, now. Don't know where that time went. Twins, a boy and a girl. Well, I should say a man and a woman, now, shouldn't I? Becky is an accountant, followed me down the same path for her sins and Josh is a PE teacher. They both live with their partners. Becky's in London and Josh is in Portsmouth"

"Are you close?"

"Yes, I would say so. They've always been my priority so even though I worked I put a lot of my energies into them when they were younger. It was just as well, really…" her voice trailed off but at that point a waitress turned up and she was able to change the subject to what she would eat.

"I think, I am going to go for the vegetable curry, please?" she said mentally counting calories. That was mostly vegetables and rice was more water than anything else. If she had no pudding her calorie count would be fine.

"Steak, please. Well done." Steve went for the predictably masculine option. The waitress checked their drinks and scurried off. "Why did you say that it was just as well?" Steve was curious.

Laura had hoped he hadn't noticed and had no intention of discussing her less than satisfactory marriage with him. She bluffed.

"Oh, no real reason. Stephen worked a lot so I was left with the bulk of the child care. Just the way it was." She tried too hard to be offhand and hoped he didn't notice.

"Aren't all women? They make out they want help from their men but they don't really. They love being in charge" Steve grinned as if he had said something funny.

Laura wasn't sure whether he was joking or had slight misogynistic tendencies. She smiled thinly and changed the focus on to him.

"What about your kids. You've got two, haven't you?

"Yes. They're in their early thirties now. Grace lives with her boyfriend and two kids each from different partners and not the one she is living with now and Darren has just left his girlfriend and baby for a nubile swimming instructor. I'm very proud!" Steve was sarcastic. He did love his kids but they also exasperated him. The university education he had poured money in to seemed to have counted for nothing and, in comparison to Laura's apparently neat and tidy family life, left him feeling ashamed.

"Oh, they can all drive us a bit nuts from time to time" Laura countered politely.

The food arrived and they began to eat. Laura felt slightly self-conscious but Steve cut into his steak and started chewing as if he hadn't eaten for a week.

"So, what do you do?" Laura jabbed her fork into a piece of butternut squash and popped it in her mouth. "Crikey – that is spicy". She waved her hand in front of her mouth to emphasise the heat of the food. She knew what he did but wasn't going to let him know that she had been semi-stalking him for most of his life. Not that she had had to do a lot of that. Her monthly phone calls with Jane provided Laura with all the gossip from the local town with minimal interjection. Jane spread gossip like rose petals on a honeymooner's bed never worrying about where it all ended up once it had come out of her mouth.

Steve played it down "Banking. It's okay".

Laura looked unimpressed so he decided perhaps he had better play it up a bit. He didn't want her thinking he was not a potential good catch. Not at his time of life. He was putting a lot more effort than he really wanted to bother with into a chance of a relationship and he didn't have time to blow it.

"I started at the bottom. You know, counter clerk when I left school then worked my way up the ladder so I'm a senior manager, now" he said airily. "Not so interesting, though. All board meetings and signing documents". He glanced at her as he forked chips into his mouth hoping that she would look impressed. It was difficult to tell. Mildly, he supposed.

"What do you do?". He had heard that she did accounts or something probably in a local garage. He assumed her apparent wealth came from a decent life insurance policy on her husband or a deceased daddy.

"I'm a senior executive at Harris and Harris. The auditors. Have you heard of them?"

Steve nearly swallowed a chip whole. Yes, he had heard of them. They were the most prestigious accountants in the area and if rumour had it soon to be merged with one of the big six.

Two thoughts flashed through his brain like race horses pushing each other out of the way in order to be the first past the post. This is the one for me, won by a short head, followed swiftly by how did she manage to do so well? He voiced that thought, curious but not sure if his ego was going to want to hear the answer.

"Good A levels. Degree in accountancy at Sheffield University. Finance Director father who pointed me towards the right companies to apply for. Short skirts, low cut tops and bobs your uncle – plenty of promotion". Laura kept her face straight.

Steve started off nodding in agreement, a studious look on his face. Yes, he expected the good education and benevolent daddy stuff but then he was surprised at what he heard. He looked up and Laura's eyes were merry. She was teasing and he couldn't help but laugh.

"So, you didn't have to do any work? Just flash your bits and up the ranks you went?"

"Yes, that's it! We women must use what we have available to us". Laura's tongue was so far in her cheek she wasn't sure it would come back out again. "Don't tell me you never did that".

"Well, I have be honest. Once I was sure I caught the Chairman looking at my bum and then lo, 3 years later I got promotion. I put it down to that".

They were laughing now, companionably, like they had 40 years ago at school when Laura had thought they were friends and Steve had not. It sobered her up. She didn't want to get involved with this man. He had hurt her, very badly. But, she reasoned, he had also made her what she was. One could argue that she owed him a debt of gratitude. His scathing words had made her think about her life. She had forced herself to get a good education convinced nobody would want her and knowing she had to do something with her life. She had brutally examined her looks and her figure and made changes that ultimately gave her some body confidence. Would she have ever done any of those things if she had not had a big wake-up call? If she had stayed tied to her mother's aprons strings, living a small-town life, marrying the first man that looked in her direction? Of course, she also had some sort of OCD, all the years of calorie counting and over-exercising had taken its toll and she couldn't look at food without worrying what it would do to her figure. That, she knew, did not come from an undisturbed mind. Then there was one other consideration despite her decision immediately after Steven's funeral that she would never, ever get involved with a man again, she wanted to because despite everything his proximity alone sent an erotic charge through her. Something that she hadn't known she was capable of feeling. Another thought came into her head, had she done all of this because one day she hoped she would be what he wanted and now that time had finally arrived? Her 15-year-old younger self invaded her thoughts with a snarky comment.

-He treats you like crap, turns a smile on you and you welcome him with open arms?

-No 55 replied calmly.

-He's had dozens of failed relationships. Do you want to be another one? Then how are you going to feel?

-Hardly dozens!

-He is a cruel, unkind man and is just going to hurt you.

-He's changed. He's been nothing but chivalrous to me since we started seeing each other.

15 stomped off, grumpily, to the inner recesses of Laura's mind leaving a niggling feeling of what if she is right, hanging in her head.

Unbeknown to Laura, Steve was having similar thoughts about a potential relationship although they were rather more straight-forward. Something along the lines of this woman would do very nicely for the rest of my life, she has looks, money and an added bonus of a sense of humour. Thank you, God and Dad, in case it was something to do with you!

"I take it you were visiting the grave of your husband?" Steve asked. They had finished the mains and Laura had been persuaded into a sweet. She chose a lemon sorbet – mostly water – she reasoned to herself. "What happened to him?"

Laura had to hide her irritation. The accident had been in all the local papers alongside the local MP's view on homelessness and a local couple's diamond wedding anniversary.

"Motor bike accident"

"Anybody else killed?"

Weird question! Subtext – Is she the widow of a murderer, perhaps?

"No"

"Oh, I remember now. It was in the local paper, wasn't it?"

"Yes"

Laura realised she was being very monosyllabic but Steve didn't seem to be deterred.

"How do you find being on your own?"

Laura was silent for a minute debating how much to say. Steve looked at her as if he had asked some sort of trick question and she came back to the present. Should she tell the truth that in fact she found little difference apart from the shopping bill was smaller and she had the bed to herself?

"You get used to it – you have to, you know, get on with it". She didn't tell him that being on her own was normal on every level instead she gave her stock answer.

Whilst Steve excused himself to go to the Gents. Laura considered what she was doing.

Her career was going well and on a good trajectory but she was definitely a 'C minus could do better' when it came to choosing partners. It was tricky, like choosing fruit in the market. The outside looked healthy and attractive but the inside could be bruised and the core rotten. The problem was that you had to bite into it to find out. What would Steve be? A crisp, juicy apple or a tasteless dried out Satsuma?

Despite it being Laura's invitation, Steve, chivalrously insisted on paying so, feeling guilty, and ignoring every warning bell in her head, Laura invited Steve to dinner at her house on the following Friday evening.

Chapter 22 – Fifty-five

As Steve walked away from the railway station on the Friday night, he wasn't sure what to expect. Memories of getting off the train at 7.30 and making his way back to his family and congealed dog food in the microwave crowded his head. He could not bear the thought of living in all that chaos and squalor ever again. He very much hoped he was not walking into the same thing.

The front door was ajar as he walked up the drive, 20 minutes later, still wearing a suit and tie, although he had loosened the top button of his shirt. He knocked gently and called out jokingly "Honey, I'm home!"

Laura laughed and called out for him to come in from what he presumed was the kitchen at the end of the hall. There were doors leading off either side, he glimpsed a lighted lamp turning a small room into a cosy lounge with cream sofas and colourful throws. The house was serene and simply and tastefully decorated, there was nothing on the stairs except carpet and nothing on the banisters except varnish.

As he walked softly on the thick pile carpet towards the end room, he could hear jazz music playing quietly. His musical tastes were not very sophisticated extending to Def Leppard and Meatloaf with a secret liking for Abba. He had no idea who the saxophonist was but the music created a laid-back vibe and he felt himself relax. The aroma of chicken in some sort of sauce, again he didn't know what it was, drifted on the air and made his stomach rumble with hunger. The room turned out to be a south facing kitchen/diner which was light and airy. The balmy evening air streamed in the open patio doors through which he could see clean wooden decking brightened up with colourful, overflowing pots of flowers. At the side of the neatly mown lawn was a wide path which started at the side of the drive and led to a very large shed at the bottom. A crisp white cloth covered a table set for two and on it were a green salad, cruet, two wine glasses, napkins (napkins!) mats and cutlery. The room was tidy and had a minimalist quality to it, the surfaces were clear apart from a bread board and a few utensils that were in use. The walls were a pale apricot shade which created an air of warmth and against the back wall a book case stood, crammed tidily with titles from Dickens to Marian Keyes. He knew without going any further into the house that the beds would have clean sheets and there would be fluffy white towels neatly folded in the bathroom. He also knew that this was not done for his benefit, this was how Laura lived and at that point he knew that this was how he wanted live. This was how he had always wanted to live. He would happily leave any vestige of his old life behind without a second glance to belong in this world.

Laura watched this man that she had yearned for all of her life walk down the hall to her kitchen and an emotion she barely recognised made her catch her breath. In her mind's eye she was back in the classroom watching as he rushed through the door with a minute to spare, shirt tails hanging out, tie askew, satchel half open sprinting down the aisle between the desks to the one in front of hers throwing a grin her way before turning his back as he slumped onto the chair. Her heart started pounding and a feeling of pure desire coursed through her. All these years she had waited and of all the scenarios she had played in her head she had not expected any of them to come to fruition. Now she was nervous, she'd been glad of her busy day to take her mind off of this moment because in truth she didn't know how to react and didn't want him to recognise the foolish school girl she had been and change his mind. These thoughts made her almost helpless and she hoped they didn't show in her face as she crossed the room to greet him.

Steve thought Laura looked fantastic, casually chic in light blue linen trousers and navy shirt with the sleeves rolled back showing lightly tanned arms, an oversize leather strapped watch and manicured finger nails. As she got close enough to kiss each other on the cheek he could smell the vanilla tones of her perfume. The touch and feel of her awoke his senses, so that every nerve ending felt as if it was on fire. He suddenly felt overawed by the whole experience, the house, the evening and most especially the woman but he couldn't let it show. He had to remain cool so decided on his usual tactic. Open and friendly, respectful and taciturn. Let the other person lead the conversation but appear thoughtful and engaged. It took him a lot of places and gave the impression that he was deep thinking and intelligent. In truth it hid his vulnerability and fear of being discovered as a fraud.

As they stepped back from the greeting each of them conscious of a frisson in the air Laura rushed to be the first to diffuse it. It was far too soon, she told herself even though her body was telling her that it wasn't, so she opened the fridge door and pulled out a bottle of lager, deftly removed the top and handed it to him with a smile. As he reached for it their fingers touched and the tension was back, a jolt of electricity leapt between them causing their eyes to meet and hold for a second longer than was necessary. So much for diffusion! Laura flushed and turned away to disguise her discomfort.

"I expect you need that after work and battling the British Rail system. Come and sit at the breakfast bar" she indicated a white leather stool "while I finalise dinner. It won't be long – 10 minutes or so! How was your day?"

Steve took off his jacket and tie and unbuttoned his shirt a little more, then perched on the bar stool as requested, bottle in hand. He took a couple of swigs while Laura busied herself with warming plates and cutting up a French stick, pieces of which she put in a basket on the table. He thought he had died and gone to heaven. All those years dreaming of Friday evenings like this. No shouting, no loud music, no sulky slovenly wives. He could not believe what was happening to him. This is what he was meant to come home to, this was it.

"Same old, same old!" he said airily. In fact, it had been a hard day full of difficult meetings, stubborn staff and endless emails. The only thing that had kept him going was knowing that at the end of it he had dinner with Laura to look forward to. "What about you?". This was a first, he thought, me asking what somebody else's day had been like and actually giving a damn about the answer.

"Oh, started off okay, met new clients which went well. It didn't end so good when one of my staff had a heart attack in the stairwell rushing to get home for his toddler's party".

"Crikey, really? Is he okay?"

"Yes, thankfully he's fine. Well, as fine as you can be after a cardiac arrest. One of the first aid team found him really quickly and called an ambulance. He's fine now and even got home in time to see his little girl smear Hungry Caterpillar cake all over their new sofa".

Steve smiled.

"That's good news. Did he have to be resuscitated or was he not that far gone?"

"Thankfully not unconscious otherwise as I was the first aider, it would have been me trying to keep him alive. Not that he isn't cute but there is a time and a place for mouth-to-mouth contact". She could laugh now more out of relief than anything else. Finding Adam slumped nearly unconscious had shocked her and on the drive home she had started having flash backs about Steven. Not about his death but the good times because there had been some despite their differences. It was guilt, she knew that. Her husband had always been second best to her and she desperately wished he hadn't been. No wonder he had retired to the shed with his bikes. He must have realised early on that he was never going to be what she wanted. She wondered what he would have thought of her entertaining the love of her life now. She didn't want to go down that route. It was pointless and her husband was gone so she had to make the most of the time she had left. Keep talking, 15-year-old Laura, inconveniently popped into her head, that's right convince yourself that you're not a complete fool! She was glad she had the dinner to focus on when she got home and even happier when she received the text from Adam saying he was much better if a little annoyed that he had to get his sofa dry cleaned.

Steve was impressed. Was there no end to her talents? A first aider despite her lofty position in the company. That was dedication over and above the normal call of duty.

Laura heaved a steaming dish of coq au vin out of the oven, kicking the door closed behind her with her heel, and ladled a serving each onto two plates. It smelt divine and Steve felt ravenous.

"Let's eat before it gets cold. This is my signature dish and the one and only thing that I can cook decently" Laura said as she moved the hot plates to the table.

Steve very much doubted that. Laura moved around the kitchen with an ease bourn of knowing exactly what she was doing. The food was delicious as he knew it would be. They chatted amiably about work then items in the news including the sacking of a football manager. Buttering a piece of French stick, Steve asked.

"Do you remember Al? My mate from school, we still see each other even after all these years."

Laura went cold. She had dreaded that this subject would come up and couldn't help herself from answering curtly.

"Yes"

Something in the tone of her voice made him glance up from the last piece of chicken he was cutting, sensing a change in Laura's mood. She was determinedly gazing out into the garden and refused to catch his eye. Steve was unsure what had happened so ploughed on.

"He used to captain a football team in one of the local villages. They did quite well at one point.

Ended up in a lower league final at Wembley. I went to watch. It was a good day out".

Laura stayed quiet. Steve was puzzled. "He's nice" he ventured in case it was the characteristics of Al's personality that were the problem. "Been married to Sandra for donkey's years but he tells me they are still happy. We could meet up with them for a drink if you fancied it". Laura returned her gaze to him and her face told him that he had said totally the wrong thing.

"Are you ok? Have I said something wrong?" Steve, put down his cutlery and wiped his mouth on a napkin – certainly not something he had done at home before – and looked at Laura. He did not want this perfect evening to go wrong.

This is it, Laura thought, she knew the time would come when they had to address the elephant in the room but she had put off thinking about it because she didn't know how she was going to do it. Did she bring the subject up herself or wait until an appropriate moment arrived? She had her answer, the time was now and she didn't want to cross that bridge. She wasn't ready. The man who had inflicted the pain was here, a different person, in her kitchen right now and she didn't want to ruin things. She was the one who had had to live with it and she decided, there and then, that she would carry on doing so. It may be the wrong thing to do but in the heat of the moment she decided to accept that it was in the past and they had both moved on. She would let it go and hope that she wouldn't regret it.

The pause was long and interminable. Laura knew it was down to her to normalise things before they got out of control. She forced herself to smile benignly as if to signify no harm done then said with finality in her voice "I prefer not to talk about school. It doesn't hold good memories for me".

Steve, did not immediately pick up on her tone but the smile was unmistakably false.

Unsure what to say he tried to ease the tension. "Okay – well we don't have to. That's fine. Let's talk about something else."

They resumed their meal in uncomfortable silence. The chill in the room met the cool air now spilling in through the open doors. Even the music had stopped as if it sensed the mood. The clock ticked loudly.

The atmosphere was too much for Steve and his voice cracked the air like lightning. "What could have been that bad?"

Laura struggled to know what to say. Steve didn't seem to be able to read the situation at all and his lack of acumen concerned her.

"I, um, I was bullied" she said very slowly.

"You were?" Steve seemed genuinely startled. He couldn't imagine this confident woman being picked upon by anybody. The morning that Laura had emblazoned in her memory barely registered in Steve's. He had never considered himself a bully but a person that held his own and justified some of his unkinder actions as self-preservation. The law of the jungle, survival of the fittest that sort of macho bullshit. A lot had happened since school and his recollections were vague and generalised. "I'm sorry about that". He added lamely.

Laura wasn't sure whether he was apologising for what he had done or uttering meaningless words in the way people felt they should on hearing bad news. She hoped for the former but knew it was the latter. She didn't want to hear any more, so got up and to hide her discomfort briskly cleared the table, tapping the CD back on as she passed it. John Coltrane's tenor saxophone instantly filled the air and she felt a little better. The evening not quite so sour.

Steve could feel the promising night disappearing through his fingers, too, and felt the familiar feeling of Friday evening anti-climax that he had throughout his marriage. He wanted to turn it around. Had to turn it around. He was not prepared to let his opportunity of happiness slip through his fingers. Chivalry was needed. He rose from the table and as Laura reached for a dish gently took her hand, lifted it to his lips and kissed it.

"That was school and this is now" he said gently "come and sit down".

Laura was struggling with her emotions and the unexpected tenderness threw her completely. It took all her inner strength not to dissolve into tears and fall into his arms. Both the shame and the longing pent up for so many years threatened to overwhelm her but she could not and would not let it happen. She was not, definitely not, going to show weakness in front of this man. She tried to protest.

"I was just tidying up. I'm fine, honestly".

"It can wait" He took charge. "Come and talk to me. About anything you like, just sit with me for a minute".

Laura allowed herself to be led back to the table by the fingertips. She sat. She didn't know what to talk about, her mind was full and empty all at the same time. They gazed at each other in the half light. Laura worked her way around his face with her eyes. The blonde, greying hair brushed back from his face, the small laughter lines around his concerned blue eyes, the straight nose, thin upper lip and the start of stubble. She didn't want to talk to this man she wanted to take him up her stairs, throw him onto the bed and have wild pornographic sex then wake up entangled in his arms in the morning. She had to get a grip. She wanted the man but it was going to be on her terms when she felt in control.

They continued to gaze at each other and the atmosphere crackled with sexual tension.

"Would you like some dessert?" her voice was husky.

"What is it?" Steve didn't take his eyes from hers.

"Cheesecake!" Laura was deadpan as she held his gaze. She wasn't a fan of innuendo but she knew it would work this time. She wasn't going to sleep with

Steve that night. She had waited many years and she would wait a little bit longer.

Steve laughed out loud. He had no idea what was going on in her head but he caught a brief look she gave him that was unmistakeable. It was pure lust he had seen it before and usually acted on it as soon as he could. When he had been married, when he had been single, it hadn't mattered. This time was different. This time he would wait until the time was right, too much was at stake.

At around 10.30 Steve excused himself. The cheesecake and the wine had lightened the mood again and he entertained Laura with some self-deprecating stories. She was amused by them. As he got up to leave, he held his hand out to her, she accepted it and stood up. He looked into her eyes, thanked her for a lovely evening and kissed her on the cheek. It had taken him many years to know how to treat a woman but this was the one he wanted more than any before and he was going to do it right. Somewhere in his subconscious he knew that if he wanted Laura, he would have to woo her and treat her with respect. It was not something he had consciously thought about before but this time the prize was worth the effort.

Chapter 23 – Fifty–five

Al was propping up the bar when Steve dropped into the pub on Saturday evening. He had called Laura in the morning to thank her for a lovely evening and to ask if they could meet up again. She had agreed to a cinema trip on the Wednesday evening, work permitting she had said, week nights were tricky as she never knew what time she was going to finish. Steve, knowing he would have to make some excuse to catch an earlier train, went along with her plan even though he was yearning to see her sooner.

"You want another?" Steve nodded at Al's nearly finished pint.

Al looked ruminatively at the glass then at the clock behind the bar. "Go on then, Sandra will still be watching that God-awful dance programme and won't miss me for another half an hour, I'm sure".

"Two pints of Carling, please" Steve called out to the bottle-blonde and buxom bar maid who brandished two glasses and started expertly filling them from the taps. A few years ago, he would have made a leery comment to Al and followed her with his eyes as she bent over collecting glasses and wiping the tables down. Tonight, she didn't interest him at all.

"How are you doing?

"Not bad, you?"

"Pretty good actually" Steve smirked.

"That sounds like there's a woman around again" Al glanced at him "Who is it this time? Not Mandy, again? You've been around that block once too many if you ask me".

"Not Mandy, no."

Al looked at him with a hard stare.

"It's not! I promise you. It is somebody much better than her."

"Keep your voice down, half her family are in this pub and you were happy enough when she was doling out free goods when you and Lorraine hit a sticky patch".

Steve shuddered at the mention of his wife's name.

"I came out for a quiet drink with my pal not to be reminded of my past bad choices, thank you". He took a swig of his pint.

"Go on then tell me who it is – I know you're dying to". Al sighed deeply.

"Her name's Laura".

"Laura?" Al's mind worked searching for Laura's that he knew. A light bulb came on and he remembered one. "Not Laura Knowles?"

"Yes, that's the one"

"Laura Coombes from school?" Al was incredulous "that Laura?".

"Yes, that one!" Steve couldn't understand what was the matter with his friend "what's your problem with that? She looks great, nice car, good job."

"Really" Al was sarcastic. "but has she actually got anything going for her?"

"She's clever, funny and interesting" Steve ignored the jibe.

"One with a personality – that's a first for you".

"We can't all be lucky with our first choice and stay with them for ever and ever, amen, like you, Al". Steve was snide. He thought the idea of staying with one woman all your life pretty boring. At least he had but he realised it depended on who it was. Paul Newman had a point!

Al had been Steve's best friend since primary school when they had been paired up in Mrs Lawrence's class at the age of 5. They had sat next to each other all the way through to secondary school where they were in the same form although not always the same classes as Al's abilities were definitely more on the practical side than Steve's. Al had been one of the ones playing football when Lorraine had set her honeytrap for his friend and he had watched him walk right into what he knew would be a disastrous relationship. Al knew about Mandy and Al had also been on the school landing on the mortifying morning for Laura. Despite what she thought, he hadn't laughed and he hadn't run off joyously. He had watched the innocent girl walk up the stairs straight into a cruel and abusive ambush and that was the first time in his life when he could have cheerfully throttled his friend. Steve's vicious attack had been for no other reason than to make him look big in front of his gang of friends. He had given no thought at all to the recipient of it. It pained Al, greatly, that Laura tarred him with the same brush as the others but there was nothing, he could do about it. He should have disowned Steve at the time but he was too spineless. He hadn't wanted to be left on his own, kicked out of the cool gang and treated as an outsider so he put his head in the sand. A decision he had regretted ever since.

He did not rise to Steve's bait, instead he said,

"Is that a good idea? Don't you remember what happened at school?"

Steve was starting to get annoyed with Al's responses now. He had expected a lot of back slapping, pint downing and general rowdiness as celebration not this weird moodiness.

"Remember what?" He asked crossly, he supposed he would have to play the game.

"What you said to her? That morning? You called her fat and ugly and dumb or something like that!"

Steve thought it was going to be something terrible.

"You know I barely remember anything about school – how many times have we talked about this? Do you remember what Mick said to Mr Brown that morning in History in the 4th year, you say and I say No, I don't remember anything about school so you end up telling me the story. Your memory is super human compared to mine – what can I say".

Al controlled himself. "You were pretty mean to her"

Steve was flippant "If I was then she doesn't remember. So that makes two of us.

We were kids – that's what kids do. I'm sure if she had she would have said something by now. Anyway, I really like her and am going to do the right thing by her so you don't have to worry".

Not trusting himself to say anything else for a minute Al drained his pint, swallowed slowly, said pointedly "You better had", then put his empty glass on the towelling beer mat and walked out of the pub without a backward glance.

Chapter 24 – Fifty-five

Lying in bed the following morning Steve knew he had not been strictly truthful with his best friend because after Laura's reaction the night before he had thought hard about school and as if a fog had partially lifted, he had a vague memory of that morning. He couldn't remember precisely but he knew he had thrown some insults at a girl in a fit of pique, fed up with being the laughing stock of his gang for having a podgy little admirer. He hadn't really meant to be so harsh but the vitriolic words had just flowed off his tongue. He added it to the list of things – many things if he was truthful – that he was ashamed of. He had been a bit of a prick at school with his showing off and general laddish behaviour. But, he justified, who wasn't? It was all part of growing up - one of the phases like treating your parents like dirt and shoplifting from the local store. It hadn't meant anything. Look how close he and his dad had been for all those years after his mum had died. Not once had Keith reminded him of his selfishness, he had only ever been a support to him. He couldn't say the same for his brother though, they hadn't fallen out as such but they had nothing in common so barely spoke.

Steve was sure that if Laura remembered she would have mentioned it last night when she had the chance but he would be on his guard, just in case. She must have been talking about something else that had affected her badly not a bit of teasing. If she mentioned anything he would apologise profusely, say he thought she had been somebody else … No, he wouldn't say that. That was really stupid. He would just have to blag it, if, and he hoped not, the subject ever came up.

The problem was that despite giving it some serious thought on the train to work and on the train home from work for many days, he could not get into his head that the Laura he knew now was the, how should he put it, immature teenager that he had known at school. He knew she was older and had a few lines and wore make up now and stylish clothes but, in his head, they were two different people. 15-year-old Laura and 55-year-old Laura. Entirely different.

Laura thought of them as two different people too and frankly, the 15-year-old was starting to get on her nerves. She wanted to dump her. Every time older Laura started thinking nice thoughts about her and Steve's burgeoning relationship there was 15 putting the kybosh on it. It was really annoying.

Surprisingly Laura had managed to finish at a reasonable time – if you call 6 pm reasonable, climbing up the ladder had meant more hours despite the promise of less – and met Steve at the cinema. Just for a minute as she waited on the steps, she had a flash back to her salacious relationship with Marcus but this film was nothing like the sort of films they used to watch. All that type of stuff had gone on line now and cinemas only showed wholesome (if you counted blood and gore) fare. Steve ran up a bit late, full of apologies about a delayed train. Laura waved them off. They grabbed a hot dog, large drink and bag of sweets (none of which Laura would eat) and took their seats in the semi-darkness. 'The Accountant' was a wry choice for Steve and starred Ben Affleck so Laura couldn't say No. They both enjoyed it.

Laura, once again, invited Steve for a meal on Friday night and knowing what this meant, Steve jumped at it. Not that he was ever going to say no. In fact, he couldn't wait for the end of the week knowing that no matter how difficult or stressful it had been, getting off that train meant walking into the world of peace, calm, organisation and relaxation.

Once again, the door was ajar so Steve made the "Honey, I'm home" joke into their little thing. Laura appreciated it. The meal was Boeuf Bourguignon with jacket potatoes and vegetables. It was, as had the meal before been, delicious. This time he noticed that Laura didn't actually eat a lot. She chose carefully what she put on her plate and took nothing else. She also drank one glass of wine, slowly, then took to water. Dessert or as Steve knew it, pudding, was lemon cheesecake – home made and he had two helpings. Laura had a few mouthfuls then declared herself full. They sat together, with cups of tea, listening to the change of mood from the jazz trumpet (Miles Davis, Laura had answered to Steve's enquiry. Was he a jazz fan? No, he decided to be honest, but perhaps he hadn't been listening to the right music because he liked this. Good, responded Laura, because it is all I ever play). Steve could get used to this level of sophistication. He had been born for it. As Laura got up from the table and leant over to clear the plates Steve placed his hand on her forearm in order to stall her then kissed her gently on the mouth. She bobbed up, surprised and looked into his eyes then looked away but not before he had seen the flame of desire that he had lit.

Laura had not expected it to happen when it did but she knew it was inevitable. Until then Steve had been solicitous barely touching her but tonight, he had made his move and Laura could not contain her feverish longing any longer. She had never known what it felt like to want a man as much as he wanted her. In her head Marcus and Steven had taken her to bed for sex and it had been fine when she got there but it wasn't the same as this feeling of hot, hot yearning that was now overwhelming her. This was passion and sex. The other men had never been the one she had wanted. The one and only man she had was in her kitchen giving her a look that said he couldn't wait another minute to get her in to bed and she realised neither could she. Out of the blue 15 popped into her head. Are you really going to do this? What if he humiliates you again? Shut up said 55 as she and Steve raced up the stairs. You're a fool, sleeping with him will be the worst thing you can do, said 15 belligerently. Goodbye, said 55.

Steve had been right. The bed had clean white sheets that smelt of summer meadows. The sparkling en-suite bathroom had fluffy towels in abundance folded neatly just waiting to be used and extra toilet rolls just in case. The place was like a hotel or at least no home he had ever lived in. The part of upstairs that he saw was as tasteful and minimalist as the rest of the house with thick piled carpets and polished surfaces. Not that he took any of that in on the first night. After their first real kiss and the meeting of their eyes there was only one place they were going to end up and they did so very rapidly.

Laura woke early and for a minute was disoriented by hearing somebody else breathing. It had been a while since it had happened – nearly two years, in fact. She lay for a while listening to the rhythmic inhalation and exhalation of another human being and marvelled that after all the years of, and she would call it what it was, craving she had finally got to her destination. Was it worth it? 15 tried to disturb her self-congratulations but 55 was having none of it. Yes, she said, unconvincingly, of course it was. Every single minute. Of which there hadn't been many but nevertheless, yes all of them! She had to admit that the heat she had felt between them had not transferred into the ardour she had thought it would. Steve had been a considerate but routine lover. He hadn't ripped all her clothes off or thrown her onto the bed. He had used the bathroom whilst she stripped down to her bra and knickers. He had taken his shirt and trousers off then climbed into bed. Once there he had rolled on top of her and started by kissing her mouth then worked his way down, down until she thought that she would melt under his touch when he had stopped and she had had to breathe in his ear not to. He had entered her and climaxed quickly then rolled off and lain limp like a rag doll. Within minutes he was gently snoring and Laura had a feeling of something she couldn't quite define.

After her exercise, on Saturday morning she went back to bed and they had a leisurely morning when there had been more 'minutes' than the first time. In the early afternoon after Laura had spoken to both children, individually on the phone, and Steve had popped home for some casual clothes, they walked to the cemetery together and did their duty at the graves. They hadn't walked hand-in-hand but so close that when they met Sally and her husband the look of shock on her friend's face told Laura everything. She knew that within minutes of being in the door Sally would phone Jane and by Monday morning her 'rose petals' would be spread across the whole town.

Chapter 25 – Fifty-five

The dates a couple of times a week became a regular thing then increased to three times a week. The relationship, because that is what it had become, happened without Laura realising it although, she told herself, she could stop it at any time. If she wanted to. She and Steve got along like they had before. They chatted easily to each other. She enjoyed his attempts to explain his sport obsession to her and he loved her dry sense of humour. Laura didn't allow him to overwhelm her. She was no longer a school girl and besotted (you might not be one but you are the other, corrected 15) so carried on with her yoga classes, tennis and meeting with her girlfriends. She was financially secure so had no need to rely on a man and was in this relationship because she wanted to be yet there was something nagging at her that she couldn't put her finger on. One night she texted Tom. They stayed in touch mostly by phone.

-Hi, how are you? How's the family? -

It took several hours for Tom to reply.

-All well. Katrine pregnant again. U ok? –

Again? Thought Laura, how many was that? What were they, rabbits?

She replied – How lovely! Congrats. All well, here. Seeing Steve Miles otherwise nothing to report –

Which was a bit like saying, the house has just burnt down but apart from that I'm fine!

This time Tom replied within 5 minutes.

-What? Seriously? Katrine says – walk away now -

Laura was not expecting that. Perhaps it was a joke.

-Seriously? -

-Seriously -

Laura – Thought they split amicably? -

Tom – She lied! -

Laura – Age difference? -

Tom – No -

Laura – Why then? -

Tom – He's cruel -

Laura – He's changed -

Tom – Keep on believing that! -

Laura didn't reply. An hour later Tom texted again.

- Here if you need me! Xx -

Laura replied with 'XX'. She didn't want to fall out with Tom even though they weren't close any more.

Laura decided that she would introduce Steve to her children. It would be a good test. If they liked him then she would feel a lot happier. Steve agreed readily, he thought that winning them over would be a good step in the right direction.

Shopping was required and Steve offered to go along, too. This was something he had never contemplated with Lorraine and as rarely as possible with Katrine but he did not want this relationship to develop into something from the 50's and secretly realised that he had been wrong all those years ago. He couldn't help it. That was the way he had been brought up but times had really changed. He had no hold over Laura so she had to be in the relationship because she wanted to be and he had to make sure that she did want to be.

At the large supermarket they decided to split up. It would be quicker and Laura hated shopping at the best of times. She saw it as a waste of her precious time when she would prefer to be doing something more interesting. Steve volunteered to get all the veg and fruit whilst she went down to the dry goods section. She had expected Steve to catch up with her but her trolley was piled high when she found him talking to a woman next door to the broccoli.

"Laura" he called out when he spotted her" Do you remember Rachel from school?"

Laura was taken aback at first. The woman looked 10 years older than both of them, was very overweight with an unflattering hair-cut and no make-up. She looked as if she had just fallen out of bed. Rachel turned and Laura realised that she did recognise her although she had changed dramatically. She was one of the 'glossies', the sycophantic girls that had followed Steve around at school and had run off laughing down the corridor on that never to be forgotten morning.

Laura was cool and polite "Yes, of course".

The woman unashamedly looked Laura up and down. She was glad that she had just had her hair done and the jeans and casual shirt flattered her figure. All the years of deprivation, hard work and exercise culminated at that point where she could literally face one of her demons with confidence. Rachel's mouth fell open and she just about managed.

"Your Laura Coombs?"

"Was Laura Coombs. I am now Laura Knowles."

Rachel looked quizzically at Steve. "I thought you…"

Steve cut her off "Really nice to see you, Rachel. Must go. Say hello to Sandy for me – might see him at the football sometime. Did you get everything?" he turned to look in Laura's trolley.

Steve put his items into the trolley, took hold of the handle from Laura and strode off leaving Rachel gaping in their wake. Laura wondered how many of the glossies she stayed in touch with and how quickly the jungle drums would start beating.

"You're a life saver" said Steve as Laura hurried to catch up.

"What do you mean? Isn't she one of your friends?"

"Rachel? No. Haven't seen her in years. Thought I was never going to get away. Lots of boring stuff about her grandchildren"

"Yet you were so close at school" Laura couldn't keep the edge of sarcasm out of her voice.

Steve missed it completely and went on "Sandy, her husband, used to play 5-a-side with me from time to time but he always had to rush back to do something with the kids. Quite honestly if I did see him, I would try to avoid him, he's as boring as her. I can't believe how she has let herself go".

Mis-reading Laura's face which was slightly aghast at the unexpected demolition of his erstwhile class mate he added hastily.

"She was never my type".

Laura bit her tongue hard in order not to say - Neither was I, apparently!!

The irony was lost on Steve.

The Saturday evening meal with Laura's twins went extremely well in her opinion. She had been amazed that they had both managed to make the first Saturday date suggested to them. Normally it took a week of negotiations to pinpoint a date a month or so in the future. She thought that their curiosity had been piqued because until recently she had been dedicated to aging gracefully on her own. Both her children although having different personalities were engaging and charming company and their partners equally so. She was proud of that fact. They warmly greeted Steve, who despite Laura's lifelong obsession, they had never heard of, made no embarrassing gaffs or talked too much about matters that would exclude him. During the conversation it was determined that Steve's children were older than Josh and Becky therefore they hadn't come into contact at school and that Josh and

Steve had played for the same cricket team albeit a few years apart. Despite the success of the evening, Laura was not comfortable enough for Steve to stay the night with her children sleeping over until Sunday so they agreed in advance that he would go home by taxi. Steve was not entirely happy about the arrangement but was in no position to argue and certainly did not want to rock the boat so went along with the plan. He wanted to argue that Laura's children were not infants and that they probably would not be shocked to find a man in their mother's bed but he hadn't. He'd been good. Lying in bed in the privacy of his flat he reflected on the evening and had to admit that he genuinely found Josh and Becky to be grounded and likeable individuals. It was another hurdle he had crossed to having a long-term relationship with Laura.

The next morning Josh and Sarah, his girlfriend, set off for home straight after breakfast. Josh had some prep work to do for his week at school and wanted it done before the match at 4pm. Sarah rolled her eyes lovingly and hugged Laura before jumping in the car and heading off.

Becky up earlier than her partner, Rob, quizzed Laura in the kitchen over green tea.

"Did you really know each other at school?"

Laura tried not to flinch and replied "Yes, but not very well".

"Did you fancy him back then?"

Laura was not in the habit of lying to her children but could not face an inquisition from her daughter who had an extraordinary way of seeing right into people's souls. At the age of 8 she had guilelessly said to her mother one day "Dad has only one love in his life and it's not me or Josh". Laura had been taken aback by the little girls' perception and had to stop herself from replying "Or me", but instead tried to reassure her that Daddy loved her very much even if it didn't always appear so.

"Like I said, I hardly knew him".

"Well, he has worn pretty well. You wouldn't know he was your age"

"What does that mean?" Laura laughed pretending to be indignant. She knew her daughter well enough to know exactly what it meant but she wasn't going to let her get away with it.

"I know your age so as far as I am concerned you are what people are supposed to look like at your age but to be honest if I was going to guess I would say Steve looks a bit younger than fifty -five."

"Says the person who thought Johnny Depp was in his twenties when he filmed the Pirates of the Caribbean films"

"I was only little, be fair" She and Becky had dropped into their normal bantering that signified the closeness of their relationship within minutes of meeting up with each other the day before. Laura considered herself lucky that no matter how little or much she saw of her children they remained close.

She was ready to jump to their assistance any time they needed something from her but equally once Stephen had died, they became her protectors and she had not had to rely on her armadillo shields as much since they had grown up. What Laura couldn't understand was why Stephen had found more solace in engines and exhausts than his own children. That question would never get answered now, and she sincerely doubted it would have had an answer when he was alive.

"Do you like him?" Laura turned the tables and tried her own interrogation.

"Yes, he seemed nice but so do serial killers when you meet them in the street"

"Becky! Honestly you are incorrigible!"

"Well, I wouldn't want to judge him on one meeting but he seemed okay. Is it serious for you?"

Laura nearly told her beloved daughter about the shadow she had lived under for so long but decided not to. She didn't want anything to influence her view of Steve.

"It could be – we'll see".

"I think he thinks it is"

"What makes you say that?"

"He kept looking at you with gooey eyes every time you left the table and he was very attentive. Dad was never like that".

"Gooey eyes? Are you sure? You make him sound like Bambi" She was right about Stephen though – he had definitely never behaved like that.

"I know what I'm talking about".

"Do you indeed? I don't want to know any more." Laura put her hand up in the stop position.

"I wasn't going to tell you anymore." Becky was picking at some strawberries and laughing "I think he might be a keeper".

Becky's enthusiastic personality always rubbed off on Laura and she laughed, too.

"You do, do you? I think you will find he was actually a forward". Laura deflected the comment.

"Ha, ha, very droll. You know what I mean".

Yes, thought Laura, I do and she is right, I always knew he was.

After the success of the meeting with her children Laura suggested they do the same with Steve's. After much procrastination which involved every excuse Steve could think of and use twice, he admitted that he didn't want to.

"Why not?" Laura asked, one evening as they settled down for the evening. Steve flicked the channels on the remote to find a football game and said

"They're not like your children".

"What's that supposed to mean?"

"They have too much of their mother in them". Probably because she brought them up Laura thought but didn't voice.

"Well, I'm sure it won't be that bad and we have to meet at some point so give it a try".

Steve acquiesced and texted both his children the next day. Robert took 5 days to reply No, thanks. His father knew better than to plead. Despite Steve's early efforts Robert had never forgiven him for leaving Lorraine and their relationship was at best strained and at worst downright hostile. Karen agreed to the meal and was told that her children were more than welcome. Steve told Laura she would only say that once. She laughed him off, how bad could 5- and 7-year-olds be?

The answer was pretty bad. This time the meal was nothing like the urbanity of the evening with Josh and Becky. The children refused to sit to table for more than the five minutes it took to pick at and complain about their food then ran around the table until Steve shouted at them to stop. He banished them to the front room to watch TV where they ground smarties into the carpet, smeared chocolate on the cushions, broke the remote control and shredded the coasters. Amidst the war zone Laura battled on dishing up home cooked food and asking polite questions of Karen and her partner, Chris, who seemed to know nothing unless it concerned Manchester United or something he had read in the Sun. Steve drank heavily as the evening degenerated and Karen refused to take the hint and go home.

Even Laura's patience wore thin as she saw the children's behaviour get worse as they got more tired and Chris refuse to down the last centimetre of his pint to draw the evening to a close. He didn't care about the kids, he told them, they weren't his. Karen laughed coquettishly as if this was some sort of compliment to her and Laura could stand no more. Through gritted teeth she cleared the table of everything, put the coats on the squirming, tearful children and thanked the surprised couple for coming. She did not add that they would see each other again soon.

Once the front door was closed and Laura was sure Karen's car had left the drive, she rounded on Steve.

"You could have warned me that I was letting myself in for an evening from hell".

Steve, semi drunk and equally angry retaliated.

"I did try to warn you. You just wouldn't listen" his face was red with anger and alcohol "Laura always knows best" he simpered maliciously.

"How dare you blame me for this. I was trying to blend – or whatever the word is – blend our families. I thought it was the right thing to do. How was I to know your children had been brought up without any sense of decorum".

"Decorum? Lorraine couldn't spell the word let alone understand it. Her parenting skills ran to Sesame Street for the alphabet and a Pampers advert for potty training".

"Then, if you knew that" Laura said quietly and surprising herself by feeling pity for Lorraine "why didn't you help her?".

Laura called Steve a taxi, despite his protestations that he could walk home and she finally had the bombsite she used to call home to herself.

Chapter 26 – Fifty-five

Steve woke up the following morning with a banging head and a pit in his stomach. It took him a few minutes to process why he had a banging head. Oh yes, too much wine and lager and, probably, vodka? He wasn't sure. Why had he drunk so much? He had been at Laura's which did not normally lead to heavy drinking. There had been other people there, he was sure of that. Then it hit him, it had been his daughter and that cretin that was her latest partner. Laura was angry he remembered that, too. He put his hands over his eyes and groaned out loud as he remembered what his grandchildren had done to her neat and tidy house. He would have to do something to rectify the situation otherwise that could be his future down the drain, but what?

Steve texted Laura a heartfelt apology as soon as he could find his phone which turned out to be in the cupboard over the bathroom sink along with a small empty bottle of vodka. At any other time, he might have thought he had had a good night! She didn't reply even when he sent a crying emoji in an attempt to put some humour into the situation although to be fair, he had to look hard to find any.

He spent the morning doing chores and watching Sky sports news. At lunchtime he wandered in the direction of the pub but still had enough of a headache not to go in. He congratulated himself on resisting the temptation and walked on past towards the cemetery. He might as well give a nod towards his father while he was nearby, he didn't have much else to do. Keith would have been mortified by the antics of his great grandchildren. He had been a mild-mannered man but out of control children and dogs, for that matter, were two of his pet hates.

As Steve neared his father's grave, he saw her. Laura was bending over her husband's headstone wiping it with a damp cloth. She had put fresh flowers into the vase that was sunk into the ground. Her hair glinted in the sun and even from a distance she looked classy with her trench coat collar turned up and sun glasses on. Steve's heart lurched in a way that he had never experienced before. This was the woman he wanted to be with for the rest of his life. He didn't care what he had to do to get her, he would do it. Paying a cursory glance towards his dead father's tomb he walked quietly over to Laura who appeared deep in thought.

"Penny for them?"

Laura swung around, glanced at Steve and without changing her expression looked back at her husband's headstone. He didn't know what he was meant to do but felt uncomfortable with the silence so decided to fill it.

"Laura, I am so sorry for what happened last night. I really thought that the kids might behave better when they were in somebody else's house. I'll pay for the damage and we won't ever see them again, if that's what you want."

Laura turned on her heel and walked towards the bench as if she hadn't heard a word that he had said. Steve wasn't sure whether to follow or not but thought that he ought to. He didn't sit close to her, the aura she was giving off was not one to be meddled with so he positioned himself at the end of the seat. The situation was messing with his head he wasn't used to being on the back foot with a woman and it disconcerted him. Once again there was silence apart from some pigeons cooing in a tree nearby and a lark trilling shrilly from way up in the sky. The noise it was making far too loud for the tiny body it came from. In the distance traffic rumbled and a siren could be heard. Steve waited expectantly until once again he could bear it no longer.

"I'm really sorry".

Laura looked towards him and in a cold voice said "I know, you've told me. Twice. You've texted me. I have read the messages. Your sorry – I get it".

Steve was taken aback this wasn't the Laura he recognised. So far, she had been warm, kind and empathetic. Now he felt a distance between them. His apologies weren't getting through and he began to feel that he was going to lose this amazing woman that he had found. He stared at her profile and saw a woman that was cool, aloof and uncaring and not somebody he recognised. He felt a chill go through him but remained fixed to the spot hoping that the person he loved would turn around and smile and everything would be alright.

After a few minutes, without turning her head Laura spoke almost dreamily.

"When you are young, you look at your parents and other adults and think that being grown up solves everything. That being young is the tough bit and once you hit that magic age of 18 your future resolves itself and lays out in front of you like the yellow brick road. But then something happens to break your heart when you are barely old enough to know that it is breakable and you are left with this vast empty black motorway that is life in front of you and somehow you have to negotiate it without a map or AA membership!".

Steve was unsure what Laura was talking about and wanted to smile at her joke but decided now was not the time. She continued.

"At the time we were out of razor blades so I had no choice but to pick myself up and get on with my life and for a while it worked. I lost weight, tidied myself up a bit, got a degree and a good job. I was doing well; I forgot that my heart was in little pieces rattling around in my chest and almost enjoyed myself for a while. Then I met Stephen.

He mistook me for somebody who could love and I mistook him for somebody who could put my heart back together. We had children and a life before I worked out that neither of us were what the other needed. He wasn't …" Laura paused, gazed into the middle distance, then continued "you and I wasn't Japanese and made of steel. At least not on the outside" she smiled thinly "made of steel, I mean, I've never been Japanese. Now he is dead, we are together and it's not what I thought it was going to be. All these years I held in my head this dream relationship between you and me because I knew that if we got together, we could make it work. I was meant for you no matter what you thought and who you were with before me but now I realise that it was a childish dream. Something I clung onto because my confidence has always been rock bottom due to a piece of cruelty I was dealt when I was at my most vulnerable. I am such a fool. All these years I have wasted chasing a relationship that is no different or special than one I could have had with anybody else".

"Laura" Steve was barely listening to the words she was saying, they were way out of his emotional range and he had no idea how to react. He could hear buzzing in his ears and a feeling of panic rose in his chest. He had never come across a complex woman before; they had never been his type but he knew that there is no such thing as a type. He had finally grown up and he wanted a relationship with somebody who had more to offer than looks. He wanted this woman who made life interesting with her opinions, her wit and her intelligence who had empathy and compassion and thought about other people besides herself. As she stopped talking, he swung off the bench and onto one knee as quickly as his fifty-something year-old legs would let him, took hold of her hand and asked in a choked voice,

"Laura, will you marry me?".

Chapter 27 – Fifty-five

One month later Steve held a coffee cup to his lips and stared out of his kitchen window at the assortment of gardens, chimney pots, rooves in various states of repair and disrepair, old bikes, new bikes and many wheelie bins for the last time. He couldn't say that he would miss that view. Today was his wedding day and after that he was going to be living in Laura's house. Laura's beautiful, well kept, comfortably furnished home. Of course, it was his second wedding day and nothing as lavish as his first. That he wasn't bothered about. Marrying a meringue hadn't worked out well for him so he wasn't remotely bothered what Laura turned up in. It could be a bin liner for all he cared, actually it couldn't, he did care but he knew he had nothing to worry about. He knew she would look stylish and elegant because she always did.

Steve swilled his mug out under the tap and decided to watch a football highlights programme he had recorded. It was hours until the wedding and he had nothing else to do. He slumped into a chair, put the TV on and searched for the recording. The familiar strains of Match of the Day started. He had to think why he hadn't watched it last weekend then realised that he and Laura had been out to a party thrown by one of her work colleagues on the Saturday evening and on Sunday had driven to visit his son in an attempt to get him to come to the wedding. Laura had been very persuasive and even impressed his new swimming instructor, girlfriend, Gail. They would both be there today.

The first match was Arsenal vs Everton and as the midfielder's cancelled each out with alarming regularity Steve's mind drifted back to his proposal and Laura's reaction at the time.

Steve had panicked – he admitted that to himself but nobody else. Laura had sounded as if he was going to finish with him and he did not want that. In the few months they had been together he had loved every minute of the time they spent together. Laura was good company and had introduced him to a way of life that he had never experienced before. It was the life that he had half-heartedly suggested to Lorraine, when he had asked her to move closer to his job, without actually believing that they would do it. They had been to a war photographer's exhibition in the city, a couple of trips to the theatre and the same to the cinema to see films that she had chosen. He had enjoyed all of it and felt that most of his life had been spent under a stone. They didn't see each other all the time so he still got to watch the sport that he enjoyed and go to the pub for a few pints with his mates. She never forced him to do anything and if he had plans, she never complained. Most of the time he changed his so that he could be with her

– anything he wanted to do could be recorded or put on hold.

At the sight of him on bended knee she had remained unmoved for what seemed like an hour. In fact, it had only been 45 seconds, but it was the longest 45 seconds of his life. He felt a grip of fear around his heart as the jeans covering his knee got damper and damper and he worried that he would never get up again when she looked him in the eye and said coolly.

"Yes, Steve Miles, I will marry you".

He didn't know why she had said his name in full like she had but he was too relieved and achy to care. He stood up with a little help from the arm rest on the bench and bent to kiss her on the lips. They tasted of strawberries and the now familiar vanilla note of her perfume overwhelmed him. Never before had he so wanted to have his life again and to treat this woman with the love and respect that she deserved. He determinedly did not think of the moment of madness on the school landing but resolved then and there to be the best person he could be on every level but especially for her.

Without telling Laura, he had had serious words with his daughter and told her in no uncertain terms that he would not ever tolerate that sort of behaviour around his future wife again. The kids might get away with it at Lorraine's house but not at his. He was surprised to find that they didn't behave that badly with his ex-wife at all and Karen took on board what he said and apologised. He was pleased with that but not so pleased when as a parting shot, she said "It's a shame you didn't care as much about us when we were growing up then maybe we would have turned out better".

Steve was shocked. He had worked long, long hours to put bread on the table and maybe didn't spend as much time with his family as he should have after all what was the point of working all week if you couldn't have a pint or two in the pub on a Sunday lunchtime then sleep it off in the afternoon? Never mind that Lorraine cooked a roast dinner every Sunday – it could be warmed up in the microwave in the same way as every other meal he every ate. At the time it had never occurred to him that, maybe he should have done more. Perhaps he should have given Lorraine a break from the kids at the weekend or taken them all out to the seaside, just for a change. If he had maybe his wife would not have got so ground down with the weight of working and managing a family. But he reasoned to himself, if she had moved to the city when he had been offered his promotion then things would have been different. She could have stayed at home, got a cleaner, they could have gone to the museums or eaten out in the evening as he had suggested. Yes, the marriage breakdown was because she just did not understand him and in the end he had had enough.

Laura woke up in the half light and groped for her phone. 5am. She could never sleep a whole night without needing the bathroom any more. It was infuriating, she thought as she padded over to the en-suite. On the way back she spotted her yoga mat and decided to get her sit ups and stretches done for the day. She had a lot to think about and organise and knew she wouldn't get back to sleep anyway. She might as well get on with her day.

As she counted her exercises, proud of the fact that she still had a relatively flat stomach at her age, thanks to a lot of hard work over the years, she pondered a conversation she had had the night before.

On the way home from her last day of work before her honeymoon she had stopped off to get fuel. She had been off site for part of the day so had needed her car. At the little shop on the forecourt where she paid for the diesel she had bumped into

Al. It was the first time they had seen each other alone since the party many years before. Laura and Steve had been invited around for dinner with Al and his wife Sandra after they had decided to get married. Sandra was petite, pretty and a bundle of loving energy and Al was clearly still besotted with her. She and Laura who knew each other by sight hit it off and after mutual compliments about each other's dress sense chatted about their children and careers. The evening had been a success and they all promised to get together again soon. Laura found their evidently happy marriage quite inspirational. Steve less so.

"They've been together since school" he whined uncharitably on the drive home "you would have thought they'd be fed up with each other by now".

Laura thought Steve was joking and from the passenger seat glanced sideways at his ruggedly handsome profile. He was looking straight ahead, thankfully otherwise they would have been in a ditch, arms relaxed but no smile playing around his lips. She was diplomatic.

"Their marriage has clearly evolved, hasn't it? They've obviously kept their family in the centre of their lives and catered to each other's needs, moving with the times. It takes a lot of work to achieve your own goals and stay strong as a family unit. You've got to want to do it".

"Do you think? He's never been with anybody else. Can you imagine only ever sleeping with the same person all your life?"

"What's the matter with that? Life isn't just about sex besides it's what you agree to in your vows" Laura was unusually sharp. "I thought this man was your best friend why are you so negative about him? Are you jealous?".

Steve had never had the harsh reality of his feelings laid out in front of him but he knew she was right. He was and always had been jealous. Whatever Steve had done in his career or with women Al had accepted. He had supported him through everything but never once envied him. He'd had no need to. Sandra had provided all the love and stability that he had required. She had so many attributes that when Steve compared them to Lorraine, he realised they were not in the same league. Al had really fallen on his feet and to an extent this had irked Steve, he wanted to have been the one with the women and the life that other men aspired to and a lot of his friends did but Al was never one of them. No way was he going to admit this to Laura. He changed his tone knowing that jealousy was not an attractive trait.

"Me, no" the big man then, looking across smiling "just think it is amazing to stay with one person all your life".

Laura had relaxed and squeezed his hand glad he wasn't being an ass after all.

Al was carrying a bunch of flowers and a large Aero.

"Oh, come on Al" Laura teased "you'll have to do better than that if you're in the dog house".

Al laughed. "No sofa sleeping for me. Quite the reverse actually she has been working so hard all this week that I thought I'd get her a little thank you present. She won't be pleased though. She's got a new dress for tomorrow and will moan about the calories!"

"Tomorrow! I can't really believe I'm doing it again. Getting married – I must be mad" Laura laughed.

Al's face changed like a cloud crossing the sun. "Then don't" he lowered his voice. "Don't marry him".

Laura wasn't sure that she had heard correctly, it wasn't what she was expecting to hear so was confused.

"What do you mean? Why not? It's tomorrow. I can't back out now?" her voice rose in pitch.

"Why not? You could." Al was fierce in a way Laura didn't expect.

"I want to marry him"

"He's not who he appears to be. He is selfish and shallow and won't treat you any better than he has treated Lorraine or Mandy or Katrine".

Mandy? Who was Mandy?

Just then a voice rang out "Al, Al I've been calling you. Keep getting your answerphone I need my kitchen rewired."

Al looked at Laura with alarm in his eyes. "Shit! I've been trying to avoid this bloke. Think about what I said". He turned around a smile plastered on his face.

"Barry – yes, sorry – been flat out, mate. Let me get my diary and see when I can fit you in".

He grinned ruefully at Laura and headed to his van with Barry in tow.

Jane turned up at 10 am to do Laura's hair full of excitement at the day ahead. She didn't stop talking from the minute she got inside the door and Laura was quite relieved when she heard cars in the drive. Her children and partners arrived at the same time, all smiles, looking smart in suits and floral dresses. It wasn't often there was such a great photo opportunity and she roped Jane in to take a family photo before she left. At 11.30 all of them except for her son headed to the registry office and they were left alone.

"Well," Josh said "you've scrubbed up nicely".

"You don't look so bad yourself". Laura was proud to be walking down the aisle on the arm of her good-looking son.

They stood in the hall waiting to go and as Laura looked in the mirror to check her hair and make-up one last time, she caught a glimpse of a framed photograph of Steven on a table. It was in his Marlboro man phase many years before when he looked carefree and handsome. He was smiling broadly and she had a guilty thought that she wished things had worked out better between them.

"Are you sure about this, Mum?" Josh checked his tie.

"I am" Laura said threading her arm through his "I know what I am doing".

Standing in the doorway of the registry office with her son by her side Laura looked at the assembled congregation. A colourful array of friends and family all with their backs to her waiting for the service to begin. She was glad they all were able to come, she had needed and wanted an audience for this. It hurt less than pinching herself over and over although cost a lot more she deduced ruefully. Ahead also facing forward was her future husband, the man she had wanted nearly the whole of her life. She could see the curls of his greying hair brushing the collar of his charcoal suit, his back so familiar to her. She thought again about her first marriage to Stephen and her naïve hope that he would exorcise all the demons of her futile longing just by having the same name. It was never going to and the more she realised their marriage was based on a fanciful premise, the more she pulled away and forced him into the garage and onto the back of the motorbike that eventually killed him. She had never admitted this to anyone but she knew it was the truth. It hadn't all been bad, of course, she had two beautiful children for which she would be eternally grateful. Lastly, as the wedding march began to play and she and Josh took their first steps down the aisle towards her new life she thought of Al's words from the day before.

Twenty steps later and she was stood at the registrar's desk alongside Steve and on the other side of him, Al. Josh gently took his arm away and stepped one pace back as Steve turned and smiled at her. Behind him Al caught her eye and she gave him a meaningful, I know what I am doing, look.

"You look beautiful" Steve whispered out of the side of his mouth.

Laura flushed slightly, took a deep breath and faced forward. The registrar stood, asked if they were ready and the service began. They had decided to write their own vows as the normal ones did not seem relevant so Laura prepared to go first.

As she turned towards her fiancé a shaft of sunlight shone through the window behind him lighting up polished floorboards, dust motes that danced in the air and illuminating the little hairs around the outside of his head like a halo. The room was instantly quiet and expectant. Laura looked at the man in front of her. The man she had saved her love for, the man she had not eaten cream cakes for, the man she ran hundreds of miles a year for. She looked into his unsmiling blue eyes and was instantly transported back to that never to be forgotten morning and with the same shock she had felt that day realised she had wasted her life on him. He was not somebody to be idolised or placed on a pedestal. He was just an ordinary man, with flaws and imperfections the same as everybody else. He could be thoughtful and he could be selfish, he could be kind and he could be cruel. And on that faraway day, he had chosen to be cruel. Cruel enough to humiliate a naïve, love-struck girl who had done nothing worse than admit she liked him. He was the reason for her loveless marriage, for her workaholic lifestyle and her endless exercising. In her eyes he was responsible for years of misery, hurt and self-depravation. She knew that what she was about to do was the right thing and her voice rang out.

"Fat, Ugly. Stupid. That was it wasn't it? That's what you called me back then. On the school landing, do you remember, Steve?" her voice was as cold as his had been 40 years before. "Did I deserve that?" she paused as Steve blanched. "I don't think so. All I ever did was like you, that was my failing but you made it quite plain that you didn't want me then so I am making it quite plain that you are not getting me now. I have wasted my life loving you and I am not doing it any more."

The registrar opened his mouth to speak then thought better of it. Instead deciding to wait to see how the scenario played out. The congregation sat motionless also waiting for the next move.

Steve looked stricken then started to bluster but guilt was etched on his face for everyone to see.

With the dignity she was not able to muster at 15 Laura turned and walked back down the aisle, her head held high. This time there was no laughter, no high spirits, no hysteria just a stunned silence punctuated by one lone voice who called out,

"You deserve better, Laura, you always did".

It was Al.

373

377

Printed in Great Britain
by Amazon